NUCLEAR CAPTAIN

Submariner Sinclair Series
Book Four

John Wingate

Also in the Submariner Sinclair Series

Submariner Sinclair

Jimmy-The-One

Sinclair in Command

Sub-zero

Full Fathom Five

NUCLEAR CAPTAIN

Published by Sapere Books.

20 Windermere Drive, Leeds, England, LS17 7UZ,
United Kingdom

saperebooks.com

ISBN: 978-1-80055-283-8

To our friends, the American submariners.
They helped us in the past; they continue so to do.

Some incidents in this book are true. All characters are fictitious, but if anyone who took part in similar wartime operations should recognise himself, the fact is coincidental and I offer my apologies.

The Author

THE SHIP'S COMPANY OF HIS MAJESTY'S SUBMARINE *RUGGED*

Lieutenant Peter Sinclair, D.S.C., R.N., Commanding Officer

Lieutenant Tom Benson, D.S.C., R.N.R., First Lieutenant and Second-in-Command

Sub-Lieutenant Ian Taggart, R.N.V.R., Navigating Officer

Sub-Lieutenant Harold Spink, R.N., Third Hand and Torpedo Officer

Midshipman Michael O'Donovan, R.N., Fourth Hand and Gunnery Officer

Lieutenant Ewan Craig, R.N., Engineer Officer

Lieutenant Geoffrey Brocklebank, R.N., Electrical Officer

Lieutenant George 'Hank' Jefferson, D.S.C., U.S.N., United States Liaison Officer

C.P.O. George Withers, D.S.M., Coxswain

C.E.R.A. Reginald Potts, D.S.M., Chief E.R.A.

P.O. Jack Weston, D.S.M., Second Coxswain

P.O. James Haig, D.S.M., P.O. Telegraphist

P.O. Rodney Slater, D.S.M., Torpedo Instructor

E.R.A. Joseph Saunders, D.S.M., Outside E.R.A.

Acting P.O. David Elliott, D.S.M., Higher S/M Detector

Leading Seaman Michael Flint, Leading Torpedoman

Leading Signalman Alec Goddard, Signalman

Able Seaman George Stack, Gunlayer and 'chef'

Able Seaman Henry Bowles, Gun Trainer

Able Seaman William Hawkins, Seaman

Ordinary Seaman Tom O'Riley, Ward Room Flunkey

Ordinary Seaman John Smith, T.I.'s Mate

S.P.O. George Hicks, Stoker Petty Officer

Stoker Patrick O'Connor, Stoker

Ordinary Seaman Leslie Thatcher, Telegraphsman and Telephone Operator

AUTHOR'S NOTE

For obvious security reasons, the correct technical ranks and rates have not been given in the nominal list. The ship's company have retained instead the titles to which they have been accustomed for so many years whilst serving in conventional submarines.

If the reader has followed Sinclair in the first three books of the 'Submariner Sinclair' series, they will no doubt make allowances for the ageless quality of those who take part in these stories. The spirit of adventure is timeless, however, and the youth of today takes over from those who were young but yesterday…

CHAPTER 1

The Barracuda

The schooner lay two miles to the north-westward of The Narrows, the tricky entrance through the reefs to Bermuda. Looking down from St. Georges, the townlet at the eastern extremity of the Bermudas, the ship was a pretty sight as she came to her anchor in the shallow waters to the north-westward of Five Fathom Hole. There was no wind and she lay motionless above the kaleidoscope of colours which the coral gave to the water. Mauves, bright purples, yellows, aquamarine and turquoise, all the colours of nature's palette danced beneath the schooner's keel.

Eighty feet on the waterline, with low freeboard and with the typical rake and sheer of the West Indies schooner, she seemed recently built. She was a handy craft, and though trim and Bristol fashion, she was obviously a working boat. Heavy sounding-gear was stowed neatly in bins on the upper deck. The sun beat down upon the teak where her crew relaxed on this drowsy Sunday afternoon.

"What are those little fish, Tom?"

The speaker was sprawled along the deck, abaft the foot of the mainmast. He half leant over the side as he gazed down at the marine life swimming unconcernedly beneath them. He wore only khaki swimming trunks, a fit and wiry young man. His pale torso betrayed him as a Briton, not long out from the Old Country, in contrast to his bronzed companion, the owner of the schooner, *Marianne.*

"The flat ones, striped vertically with yellow and black stripes?" Tom Hillyard asked.

"Yes. They look like The Wasps, but they seem to be left alone by the others."

"They're Sergeant-Majors, Peter. The other fish disregard them. Because of their friendliness, perhaps."

Peter Sinclair was in his middle twenties. His host was middle-aged, however, and difficult to categorise. He seemed as tough as the teak on which he stood and he had travelled widely by the look of him. With his grizzled moustache neatly groomed with soldierly precision there was a military air about him. The shining skin was drawn tightly across his high cheekbones but there were hollows in either cheek. He was obviously a man-of-the-world, having spent much of his life east of Suez.

Tom Hillyard was a character. Peter Sinclair had been grateful to accept this hospitable Bermudan's friendship. Life was pretty dull in 'Arcadia', the villa he and his fellow officers shared when returning from a day's exercises, and Tom Hillyard's company made a welcome break. Tom was a marine biologist in his fifties. When he was not at sea in his schooner, trawling and sounding the deeps to the south-westward of the Bermudas, he lived in a bungalow on the far side of the Town Cut. This channel through the islets connected St. Georges with the Atlantic, on the seaward side of The Narrows. Tom had run into Peter shortly after the young Briton had brought alongside his first nuclear command, H.M. Nuclear Submarine *Rugged*. The Bermudan was a bachelor, coming and going as he pleased, and sometimes disappearing for months marine surveying. He was a good friend to the newly-arrived submarine captain and his Ward Room. Both men got on well together in spite of the difference in their ages.

Tom Hillyard stood up. His shadow slanted across the drowsy submariner who had started to fish by lazily dangling a lump of bread on a jagged hook before the contemptuous eyes of a goggling rock cod. Peter looked up and saw Tom preparing his fishing spear, a three-pronged and barbed affair.

"You'll never get anything with that, Tom!" laughed Peter.

Peter saw Tom jerk his arm in a sudden movement. The spear clove the water. A circular stain welled to the surface. Tom hauled in his line carefully, and then a pink stickle-backed rock cod flopped on to the deck, struggling on the jagged barbs.

There was a hard light in Tom's eyes as he stared down at Peter.

"Not bad, eh?"

Tom smiled with his mouth only; his face creased with pleasure, but his eyes remained strikingly cold and hard, with the faraway blueness so typical of the crofter's from the Western Isles.

"Wretched fish!" Peter replied. "It must be pretty difficult to allow a correct aim-off, Tom. But you only got a rock cod!"

"De Cap'n, he sometimes get a barracuda," a voice crooned behind Peter. Joseph, one of the crew, had joined them from the fore-hatch and he was grinning as he held his arms wide.

"Yes, sah. Big as dis dey are!"

Peter smiled: it was the same the whole world over.

"I'd like to see you get one, Tom. Impossible, I'd have thought."

"It's a matter of practice. I used to stand on the bottom of a gangway at night, and the barracuda would come up to the light. I'd spear 'em as they flashed past."

"Fastest fish in the world, aren't they?"

"Yes, and one of the most dangerous. Long and narrow like a razor, they're six feet long sometimes. The fastest fish in the sea, they say. They'll attack you if they get the chance."

Peter grunted. He wanted a swim.

"Any out here on the reefs?"

The water was like crystal. Below them the underwater gardens extended in a profusion of pastel colours: branching coral ferns waved lazily, their fronds a filigree of delicate tracery, the purples of the deeps contrasting vividly with the yellows and greens, the pinks, the reds and the mauves of this coral underworld.

"No, Peter. They stick to the deeper waters of the Sound and the Dockyard area."

"In that case I'll have a dip," Peter replied. He stood poised for a moment on the gunwale, then dived cleanly into the water.

It was another world below the surface. A pity he couldn't study this coral through the periscope of his submarine! He rolled over on his side, and he saw the surface undulating above him, just as it looked through the periscope before the lens cleared on breaking surface. He expelled air through his mouth and he watched the bubbles go streaming upwards. He was overwhelmed with happiness as once again he realised his good fortune. To be given command of one of Britain's first nuclear submarines was an honour in itself, but to have the luck of being sent to this station was too good to be true! He porpoised to the surface, saw Tom grinning down at him, and took another deep breath. Peter waved and dived again, down to the wonders of this coral world.

Yes, he was proud of being recalled to duty from ashore where he was working laboriously on a Russian Interpreter's Course. Admiralty had given him little time for decision, but he was glad now that he had accepted. He had been informed of the troubles in the West Indies, but how the nuclear submarine *Rugged* was going to be used he had yet to discover. "When *Rugged*'s worked up, then we'll tell you what we want you for," the Director of Operations had said. *Well, I've finished my programme*, Peter mused, *so they'll have to do something with me soon.*

He swooped downwards, marvelling at the beauties of the coral. He glimpsed shoals of 'sergeant-majors', green and black minnows, and several angelfish, ethereal in their heavenly blue. Then he heard a tapping echoing through the water. *Like hull-tapping*, he thought. He swept with his arms and glided up to the surface.

He saw the blue sky above him. He shook his head and swallowed to clear his ears. He thought he could hear shouting. He turned on to his back and was surprised to see how far he had drifted from the schooner. *Hullo!* he thought, *what's all the panic about?*

Tom was leaning over the guard rails and waving frantically. *He wants me*, Peter thought, and he dog-paddled for a moment to try and hear what the hullabaloo was about. Then Peter caught Tom's words floating across the fifty yards of water.

"Barracuda!"

Peter followed the outstretched arm. Tom was pointing to a spot off the starboard bow, about twenty yards from Peter.

"Float on your back, Peter! Keep still. It's your only chance!"

Peter flipped round on to his back. He gently moved the palms of his hands and pointed his head towards the schooner. He felt his heart racing and for a moment he was afraid. A second of panic, a momentary loss of control, and he would be ripped open by the savage marauders. They only had to sight him or feel the pressure of a sudden shock, and they would glide towards him effortlessly — a flick of the whip-like body and the razor-sharp fish would slash into him. He swallowed as he saw Tom's outstretched hand from the corner of one eye. The barracuda were nearer now.

"I can't stand this, Tom! I'm coming out!"

Peter's nerve broke. He was impelled by a primeval fear, stronger than his will. Out of his natural element, his reason revolted. He felt his lungs sobbing as they clamoured for air. He swam frantically, disregarding all caution. His arms flailed in panic and he kicked and thrashed with his legs. He shoved his head down and struck out desperately for the schooner. Water gushed into his lungs as he gulped for air and then, for an instant, he saw Tom's white face above him. He was standing astride, one arm raised above his head, his fishing spear poised...

Suddenly Peter felt a searing pain in his groin, and something flashed past him. He felt the blood streaming, and he knew then that he had no chance: barracuda were attracted by the smell of blood, they said. He saw *Marianne*'s side less than five yards away. Desperately he hove himself from the water in a last attempt to reach the gunwale. He missed and he felt his fingers slipping down the smooth side. He lunged again as a green monster flashed towards him, less than eight yards away. He shut his eyes.

He heard a shout and felt a faint thud as the spear pierced the water. Then Peter saw the fish flailing savagely, a yard from his kicking legs. It was snapping in fury, the shaft of the spear protruding grotesquely from its shoulder. Its body writhed and twisted as it flung itself into the air in desperation. If the line snapped...

"Hup!"

Peter felt the heaving line around him and then he was dragged over the gunwale by the burly Joseph. Peter slumped to the deck. He was trembling. He was watching the reptilian creature writhing in the water that was stained with his blood when Tom came towards him.

"Your leg all right, Pete?"

Peter had forgotten about the wound and he was surprised when he gazed at the gash in his thigh. Like a razor slash it was, but longer and deeper.

"We'll soon fix you up. Weigh anchor, Joe."

Tom hauled the barracuda from the sea and threw it to the deck.

"Thanks, Tom," Peter said quietly. "You saved my life."

Tom smiled and turned away. He took the stops off the mainsail and went for'd to set the headsails. Peter felt ashamed of himself when Joseph came aft with a strip of cloth to bind the wound.

"Lee-o!"

The boom slatted across and, as Joseph deftly tied the bandage, Peter felt the schooner lift to the slight breeze. He stopped sweating and went aft to help. Tom was standing at the tiller, filling a pipe.

"You were lucky, Peter. I once saw one of the darn things go straight through a woman who had dived from the high board in Kingston, Jamaica. A ghastly business!"

The low-lying land was fine on their starboard bow and already St. Catherine's Point was abeam. In the offshore evening breeze, the aromatic scent of the cedars drifted to leeward. White houses stood boldly against their background of hibiscus, and on the small hill that overlooked the sheltered harbour of St. Georges, the whitewashed walls of 'Arcadia' stood four-square to the Atlantic. It was pleasant sailing back to their safe haven. The channel buoys were coming up fast now, and they would be rounding up soon for the Town Cut.

Peter was unconsciously trying to catch his first glimpse of *Rugged.*

"Jamaica must be a bit different now, with the Commies in control, Tom. But perhaps even they have their troubles?"

Tom was watching the luff, feeling for the wind.

"Guess so. But things couldn't be worse than when we had the island. We've been promising them a Royal Commission for years."

"What's going to be the end of all this, Tom? The Communists are virtually in control from Cuba down to the Antilles. They're even in Colombia now and can threaten the Canal."

"They've got British Honduras and Nicaragua as well, don't forget. I reckon we might as well hand them the whole of the Caribbean on a plate." Tom turned towards his guest. "Like to take her up the Cut?"

Peter took the tiller while Tom went below to start the engine. Peter rounded Number Six red and white can buoy while Joseph lowered the sails. The schooner steadied in the middle of the Cut, and Peter watched the cedars sliding by on either side. Somewhere behind these trees on his port hand lay Tom Hillyard's bungalow, with its natural anchorage running up to the green lawns.

To starboard, the shallow-pitched roofs of the old barracks appeared from behind the banks, and Peter smiled when he saw them. They had changed little over the years, but the troops liked them because they were far from officialdom at the naval base on Ireland Island. While *Rugged* had been working up, the sailors had enjoyed their freedom in St. Georges; here they learnt to live in harmony and they were especially lucky because so many of them had served together before. Peter had asked for as many of his old ship's company as possible, and Their Lordships had obliged more than Peter had believed possible. The Coxswain, Withers, and the Second Coxswain, Weston, were still with him; he had managed to trace Bill Hawkins, who had asked to remain an Able Seaman whatever else happened.

And Peter had been lucky with his officers: Benson had joined him as his Second-in-Command and First Lieutenant; Ian Taggart had been delighted to throw up his insurance job to get back to sea. Then, of course, there was 'Hank' Jefferson, the American Lieutenant of the United States Navy, "Lootenant George Jefferson, U.S.N." as he called himself. He'd joined as the Liaison Officer working between the Royal Navy and the new United Nations organisation, the U.N. Naval Security Force, which had been formed some years ago now. Wasn't that Hank's tall figure waiting for him on *Rugged*'s fore-casing?

The schooner was approaching the end of the Cut and the broad sweep of the harbour stretched out ahead as Peter took her into St. Georges. He swung to starboard to take her alongside the jetties which ran out from the town square.

Perched upon the hillocks surrounding the small square of St. Georges were the white villas and bungalows of the retired Bermudans; they had migrated to this end of Bermuda for peace and quiet. Around this square the local population dwelt, carefree among their canna lilies, happy in their palm-spangled townlet. Their natural gaiety exploded into singing, and their songs would echo upwards in the cool of the evenings. The houses on the hill would open their verandah doors, and amongst the oleanders, man and woman would listen to the refrains that lilted above the croaking of the tree frogs. Less than twenty yards from the square was an islet which had been transformed into a submarine base and which was large enough to take one large nuclear submarine or two smaller nuclears. *Rugged* lay at the jetties, one of the first Mark IIs.

Peter smiled as he assessed her with a seaman's eye. Her ensign was foul of the ensign staff and he must remember to give Number One a rocket. But she looked sinister in her black paint, powerful and efficient. The Mark IIs were a tremendous advance on our first nuclears, and he smiled as he remembered the hullabaloo over *Dreadnought.* Obsolete now, like Stephenson's Rocket, she was cumbersome in contrast to this latest nuclear, *Rugged.*

With the advance of reactor design and because of the direct transference of nuclear to electrical energy, *Rugged* displaced barely 3,000 tons; for a nation that knew how to operate small boats in restricted waters this was a godsend. Her towering conning tower, known now as 'the Fin', seemed as high as the hotel on the north side of the square, and the length of her hull bulged whale-like from the blue waters of the harbour. He could see the Officer of the Watch sending the Bosun's Mate for the First Lieutenant, and Peter smiled as he remembered his days as Third Hand of the first *Rugged.* What a contrast was this lethal weapon which loomed over the peaceful town! But this *Rugged*'s job was different: to enforce peace, not to make war.

"She's a fine vessel, Peter."

Peter nodded as he felt Tom taking over the tiller. With her nuclear power she had an immense range: she was the perfect submersible, able to stay dived for months on end. But Peter couldn't see what good she'd be out here. Perhaps she was only here to avoid prying eyes in the Clyde? He heard *Marianne*'s engine racing as it went astern, and then she slid gently alongside the jetty. Peter gathered his swimming things and then turned to thank the man who had saved his life.

"Don't thank me, Peter, for heaven's sake! It's the least we can do for you submariners. And watch out for barracuda next time!"

Peter felt embarrassed as he walked ashore. His Liaison Officer was waiting for him.

"Hullo, Hank, what's up?"

The American saluted, then spoke quietly to his Captain. Peter heard Tom calling and he looked back at his friend who was handling the warps.

"No bad news, I hope, Peter?" Tom asked.

"Just routine," Peter replied. "I've got to be at Admiralty House by nine o'clock tomorrow — another conference!"

"Poor devil!" Tom groaned. "My son Dick is at The Princess and he's plagued by conferences. That's about all U.N.O. does here — talk!"

"Oh, I wouldn't say that, Tom! After all, look at *Rugged*: we come under U.N.O.'s orders, but she can do more than talk."

"Maybe," Tom replied heatedly. "But I get s-so s-sick of watching the Commies taking all the tricks. They're winning all d-d-down the line in the C-c-carib-bean."

A peculiar look of hate swept momentarily over his face and the blue of his eyes was as hard as steel. In his anger he was stuttering, and he hurled the rope down to the deck in disgust as he stamped aft to the doghouse.

CHAPTER 2

Immediate Notice

It was one of those glorious spring mornings in Bermuda when all is right with the world. The turquoise sea sparkled and danced beneath the sun. The cardinal birds were darting in and out of the oleanders and bathing in the white dust of the road. The glare from the whitewashed walls of 'Arcadia' hurt Peter's eyes as he strolled down the path to St. Georges. He'd had a good breakfast and he was hoping for something out of the ordinary from headquarters — they'd been messing about here long enough, and, in his lethargy, he was even looking forward to their first routine docking in the dockyard. She badly needed a scrape because the weed grew fast in these warm waters. He saw the car waiting for him in the square and he cursed under his breath. What fun Bermuda had been before the advent of the motorcar! It wasn't until the war that the infernal machine had arrived with the Americans. He recalled his midshipman's days pre-war and he smiled to himself.

"Mornin', Peter."

"Hullo, Tom," Peter replied from his dream-world. "What gets you up so early?" he asked Hillyard who stood before him in the square.

"Thought I'd catch you before you left for higher society. I'm going into Hamilton later on, and I wondered if you'd care for a round of golf at the Mid-Ocean."

Peter jumped at the chance. There'd be nothing better after a conference.

"So long, Pete. See you later then," said Hillyard. "I'll try to get Dick to join us, but the cipher department is overworked just now."

Peter jumped into the taxi and waved. Tom was a good friend and had done his best to relieve the boredom. He had hinted that Peter might care to join him on his next surveying expedition off The Banks. Perhaps Peter might be able to wangle a day or two off during the routine docking, if Benson could take the weight?

The old car trundled between the oleander hedges. The road was glaring white with dust, and as the taxi reached the crest of high ground above Harrington Sound, Peter could see the dockyard well out to his right. Over to the left he even caught sight of the darker blue of the Atlantic deeps. The road curled to the north of Hamilton, the capital of Bermuda, until it reached Clarence Cove at the far end of the peninsula. The car bore away to the north and then up a short drive. Peter glimpsed the cedar trees shading the secluded headquarters of the United Nations Naval Security Force in Bermuda. This old building of oleander-covered walls was once Admiralty House and belonged to another age. His midshipman's days had sometimes been spent here, Seine-netting in the Cove below the sloping lawns. The Admiral and his gracious lady had often played hosts to the Gunrooms, and many a pleasant day had been whiled away in the blue waters of the Cove where, it was said, a green moray always lurked. They were happy days.

When he jumped from the car, a United Nations sentry saluted and politely asked him for his security pass. Peter was ushered into the anteroom where he found Hank Jefferson complete with the day's secret signals he had already collected from The Princess.

"Good morning, sir."

"Morning, Hank. All ready?"

"Yep. Let's go in, sir."

Peter and Hank sat at the far side of the table so that they could see out across the reefs. They were in for the weekly briefing, so they might as well have something to enjoy.

The Commodore was a small man, all bustle and efficiency. He was reputed to be a protagonist of the gun and rocket, rather than the torpedo and Polaris missile. Submariners were suspect, even in these advanced days; they were too often scruffy in their appearance and seemed to care little for officialdom.

Peter heard the routine announcements of shore administration and found himself relapsing into the frustration that men of action feel. As usual the seagoing was drowned in 'bumf'...

"...Serious, gentlemen, extremely serious," the Commodore was saying. "But before giving my orders, here is an up-to-date situation report:

"As you all know, the Caribbean is in a ferment, ably kept going by the Communists. They have succeeded beyond their wildest dreams, I believe. We all thought the rot would stop after they took over Cuba in 1960. We know the reason — weak leadership and our usual run of politicians. But it is easy to criticise in retrospect; let's look at the record." The Commodore cleared his throat. He glanced at the water carafe in disgust, thought better of it and took a hurried swig before continuing.

"The West lost Cuba in 1960, followed shortly by Santo Domingo and Puerto Rico, its near neighbours. The Communists then became more cunning. They shifted their attack to the Canal Zone and now Panama itself is threatened. It was Colombia's turn next. Cartagena, once sacked by Drake, is now their H.Q. and being to the eastward of Cristobal, it commands the eastern end of the Canal. Nicaragua next; and then our first loss to the Commies in the Commonwealth, British Honduras. Gentlemen, this was bad enough. Then Jamaica fell to them nearly a year ago, *entirely because of our neglect and laissez-faire attitude.*" The Commodore pounded the table. "For over twenty years they had been promised a Royal Commission, gentlemen…

"Jamaica has hit us, as sailors, worse than the others, because we have lost its refuelling facilities. By its geographical position, it commanded the West Indies and Caribbean. We have to operate from Bermuda now, by no means a satisfactory arrangement."

Peter glanced around the table. The secretaries were busy scribbling, the liaison officers were bored and the sea-going officers…? He was astonished to find that he was the only seaman there.

"Until now, gentlemen, the enemy have sheltered behind the risk of Thermal War. They have forced us back until we can no longer put off the decision." The eyes flashed and he thrust his hands behind his back. "At last the United Nations have sanctioned action by the British Section of the Naval Security Force. U.N.O. learnt its lesson way back in … where was it, Flags?" he asked his aide as he searched his memory.

"The Congo, sir, back in sixty," the young man drawled, the 'bunch of bananas' glittering from his left shoulder.

"Ah, yes, the Congo," the Commodore continued. "But the U.N. has been given teeth during the past few years. The Security Council is now a manageable body with a mind of its own and with a will to enforce its decisions. You'll be delighted to hear that today we have received orders to take action. We have been given the following mandate." The older man picked up his spectacles to peer at a pink slip of paper.

"'The British Section of the Naval Security Force is to take full responsibility for the Caribbean Area. All enemy arms, troops and agents are to be prevented from entering the West Indian Islands. All ships found so doing may be destroyed…'" The Commodore was grinning as he glanced at the astonished men around the table.

"'Fightin' talk,' isn't that what you'd call it, eh, Jefferson?" He waved the signal before their eyes.

"The miasma of Communist intrigue and infiltration has rotted all resistance in the Federation and even the police are now unreliable. Some planters have already defected, with an eye on the future. You can hardly blame them after our record of ratting on the settlers." The Commodore looked accusingly at the Secretariat as if they bore responsibility for this state of affairs.

"Well, gentlemen, I have had Top Secret Orders from Admiralty and *Rugged* has been ordered to come to immediate notice."

There was a rustle around the table. Peter felt all eyes upon him and he grinned broadly.

"Lucky devil, Sinclair!" the Commodore chuckled. "Wish I were twenty years younger." He passed a buff envelope across the table. "Here you are, my boy!" he said, his eyes twinkling. "Don't even know what's in them myself, but come to immediate notice for sea. Initial for them, please."

"Thank you, sir. It'll be a welcome break for the ship's company. May I carry on to the Ops Room, sir?"

"Yes, Sinclair, and good luck." The older man held out his hand. "Watch out in the Caribbean. It's not all it's cracked up to be."

Peter was glad to reach the cool clubhouse of the Mid-Ocean. Hank had insisted on returning to St. Georges with the message for Benson, so that Peter could enjoy the remaining few hours of fresh air. Already *Rugged* would be preparing her reactor for sea; last-moment stores and water would be squeezed into her; Taggart would be checking that all up-to-date Confidential Books were on board and…

"Hullo, Peter, sorry I'm late. I've only just finished with the bank."

"What cheer, Tom! That's all right — just arrived myself."

"The island's so full of foreigners these days that one can hardly exist on one's own island," Tom complained as he tied his spiked shoes. "There's every nationality under the sun in Hamilton, now that U.N.O.'s here for keeps. There must be an awful security risk with all this riff-raff about." He bent low to remove a clod from one sole.

"Oh, the security's pretty good," Peter replied. "But living here's your worry, Tom. I hope to be moving soon, though don't, for heaven's sake, mention it."

"Of course I won't. I've learnt to keep my mouth shut since my boy, Dick, has been working at The Princess. He's as close as a clam." Tom stamped his feet on the pitted wooden boards before moving out on to the course.

It was a heavenly afternoon, cotton-wool clouds scudding across the cerulean blue of the Atlantic sky. Peter gulped the balmy air, tinged with the aromatic tang of the cypresses. The emerald turf swept down towards the coral reefs, swung round and sheered upwards to the white prominence of Gibbs Hill Lighthouse.

Peter and Tom were both on form. The smack of driver against golf ball was music that always thrilled, and as the two friends strode downhill, the wind blowing through their open-necked and short-sleeved shirts, Peter's heart lifted at the prospect of action.

Surely he wasn't being given a free hand? He would soon know when he opened his sealed orders, and he lengthened his stride impatiently. He wanted to finish the game now and return to his boat. Preparing a submarine for sea was always worth watching — you never knew until you dived whether your trimming calculations were correct.

"Phew!" Tom complained as they left the eighteenth green. "You don't give an old man much of a chance!"

"My only hope is to exhaust you, Tom. You beat me two and one, hang it all! What more do you want?"

Tom rubbed himself down and suggested that they cancel the swim as Peter was obviously in a hurry. "Let's fetch Dick and have a noggin at the Blue Parrot before you go back."

But after waiting in the enormous foyer of The Princess, the Administrative block of U.N.O., they were told that Dick was on duty until nine.

"Pity," Peter said. "I haven't seen him for some time." They retraced their tracks to the waterfront of Hamilton, one of the most pleasant shipping termini in the world. An immaculate quay, long enough to berth one of the *Queens of Bermuda*, embroiders the one-sided street that faces the harbour. Encircled by cedar-mantled islets, their green tinged by Prussian blue, the capital of Hamilton is the heart of the far-strung Bermudas. Soft pinks and glaring whites, pastel blues, the crimson cannas, the oleanders streaming over balconies and doors, can there be a lovelier harbour in the whole wide world?

The Blue Parrot nestled in the shade, and from inside came the hum of conversation. Peter blinked when he entered the room after the glare outside. They elbowed their way to the bar and perched on cedarwood stools, while they waited for the beer, ice-cold from the cellars below.

"Cheers, Peter. Good luck."

"Cheers."

They soon found the atmosphere conducive to talk, and, before they knew it, Tom was discussing the rumours that were circulating, wild and irresponsible things, but emanating from the more mature section of the community. Tom got heated, and when he did an edge always crept into his voice. He seemed unable to control his stutter.

"I shouldn't pay too much attention to them if I were you, Tom."

"But they're t-true, aren't they? The C-commies have g-got us on the run all d-down the line."

A couple of large foreigners seemed to have cornered them against the bar. Peter felt that they were eavesdropping and nudged Tom. But as he seemed still to be truculent, Peter paid for the drinks and led the way out into the sunshine. He was grinning as he watched Tom emerge, snorting. His moustache bristled and his cold eyes seemed icier than ever.

"S-swine, that's what they are, underhand s-swine!" and he clapped the crumpled panama squarely on the top of his head. "Come on, P-Pete, let's get back to S-St. Georges and my s-schooner. These people give me the w-willies. Whose island is it, anyway?"

They jumped aboard the old diesel train as it clanked out of Hamilton, and it took the whole journey for Tom to simmer down. They climbed out at St. Georges and Peter walked down to the square with his older friend. There was much activity around the submarine, and he felt proud to be her Captain.

"Would you like to come on my next surveying trip, Peter?" Tom asked suddenly, as they leant upon the sea wall to watch the activity across the causeway.

"I'd love to, Tom, but when could I get away?" Peter was watching the tall figure in khaki drill that was crossing the bridge and coming towards them.

"What about your docking next week? Surely you could get away for a couple of days?"

"It's very good of you, Tom, but I…"

"Excuse me, sir," an American voice drawled. "Signal for you." Hank Jefferson turned politely towards Tom Hillyard. "Forgive me for interrupting, sir."

"Of course." The scientist looked down and stubbed out his cigarette in the dust.

Peter glanced at the signal. Then he turned and looked at his friend. "You'll have to excuse me, Tom. I've got a few things to do. It's been a grand afternoon and thanks a lot for the beer." He grinned and swung off across the little bridge to disappear behind the bevy of buildings of the submarine base.

CHAPTER 3

Sealed Orders

The first light of dawn was breaking when Peter climbed on to the gigantic fin. He seemed poised over the edge of an abyss as he glanced down *Rugged*'s port side, black and sleek in the twilight. The town was still asleep, and he wondered when he would see it again. He was impatient to reach his diving position twenty miles northeast of St. David's Head, where he was instructed to open his sealed orders.

"Singled up, sir," Benson reported in the darkness. "Ready for sea. All hands on board."

"Thank you, Number One. Let go aft, let go headrope. Back up the fore-spring."

A clatter on the fore-casing, a splash, and the headrope was slipped.

"Slow ahead," the Captain ordered. It was strange to give one engine movement only, and he often had to remember that she had only one propeller, though an enormous one. The fin trembled slightly under his feet.

"Stop motor."

The fore-spring came taut in the darkness and Peter watched her bows start to swing towards the pier.

"Slow astern, let go fore-spring..." and then a few seconds later, "Stop motor." There was a splash and they were free.

"Starboard five, slow ahead," he said quietly. He let her swing to clear the jetty, and then he handed her over to the coxswain.

"Take her out, Coxswain."

The quiet voice of Chief Petty Officer Withers could be heard inside the bridge as he acknowledged the order. The coxswain always enjoyed this, the moment when the beautiful creature was entirely in his hands, and he smiled in the gloom of the steering compartment as he grasped the steering-motor control. He'd often taken her through the Cut and he could do it blindfolded.

Perched on the fin, Peter felt his way across the harbour, and, when he was lined up with the middle of the Cut, he swung her towards it. As he neared the narrow causeway he felt the freshness of the morning blow through him, and he heard the whisper of the water as it lapped gently along *Rugged*'s sides.

"Steady."

"Steady, sir. Course o-eight-one."

"Very good," Peter replied when he saw that she was in the centre of the channel. He looked to his right to see if Tom, an early riser, was up yet. The first silver streaks were pencilling the eastern sky, and a weird light washed the cedars in a dead green, unnatural and cold. To his surprise, he saw Tom standing on the foreshore of the Cut. He wore an open-necked shirt and was waving a red sweater. Peter stared down at his friend who was grinning up at him.

"Better luck next time, Tom," Peter shouted through cupped hands. There was an acknowledging wave from Tom and then she had slipped by, leaving the Bermudan to watch the submarine merging into the dawn.

"That was an uncommonly friendly gesture, sir," Benson remarked. "Permission to secure for sea?"

"Carry on, please, Number One. Yes, Hillyard's been a good friend to us. I'm sorry to miss his surveying invitation; it would have been fun."

Rugged cleared the Cut and then turned sharply to starboard. By the time she had reached the Outer Fairway buoy of The Narrows, Number One had secured her for sea.

"Half ahead, course o-four-five. Take her to our diving position, Pilot. I'm going to my cabin."

"Aye, aye, sir," Ian Taggart replied dourly. He never was an enthusiast about early starts and now he had to face the ugly fact that they would be watchkeeping for weeks. He sighed as he took his last glance backward at St. Georges which was fading already behind the low-lying coral. And who would take care of Judy while they were away? There were plenty of volunteers for that duty amongst the shore staff, and he swore under his breath as he crouched over the bearing ring to take a fix.

Benson was doing the rounds of the compartments before they dived. It was vital that all loose gear should be stowed and secured properly, because these boats did everything bar looping the loop. Gone were the days of comparatively calm changes of depth; the ship's company now wore safety harness to prevent injury from the sudden swoops of this high-speed submarine.

The First Lieutenant was in the fore-ends, talking to Able Seaman Bill Hawkins. They were checking the clamps that secured the fore-hatch, which was further aft than in the conventional boat and designed to do duty both as escape hatch at sea, and as a fore-hatch in harbour, through which the torpedoes were lowered when ammunitioning.

"Had a sledge on them, Hawkins?"

"Yes, sir. They won't walk back," the burly seaman grinned. Hawkins was a thickset man in his thirties. He was rarely seen in uniform but could always be found in the Buffer's Caboose, cap tilted across the back of his head, the fair hair sprouting beneath the rim while he carried on splicing. He spoke little, preferring his own company to that of others. His blue eyes would look up questioningly, as if life was hurtful, something he did not quite understand, and then he would continue with his splicing. His messmates respected him and he was their acknowledged leader because of his age. The officers were nervous of him; he was a better seaman than most of them. There were rumours that the Captain and Bill Hawkins were old warhorses, having shared several escapades together, but the older seaman never referred to them. His messmates instinctively understood Hawkins, and they left him alone with his thoughts. He'd lost his wife and kids in the war, bombed somewhere down in the Old Kent Road. "He told the 'swain about it once," Smith had remarked.

The First Lieutenant moved on through the Petty Officers' Messes where he saw the Second Coxswain stowing his kit. The black-bearded giant looked up, and a row of white teeth gleamed in the scrub.

"Bit different to the old *Rugged* and the Med, ain't it, sir?"

Benson smiled. Weston had been unable to lie at full length in that little boat. But now he was stowing his shore-going uniform into Savoy-type aluminium lockers, while in the corner of the Mess the pearly screen of a television set glowed.

"Can't find anything to moan about, sir." The man chuckled and carried on with his stowing.

That's what I like about this life, Benson thought. *In The Trade there's an atmosphere that's friendly and disciplined both at the same time. We're all in it together and you have to know your stuff.*

He moved on to the Control Room where he found Saunders, the Outside E.R.A., going carefully over the panel.

"All right, Saunders?"

"Yes, thank you, sir; but I think there's a bit of a leak in Number One L.P. Blow. She won't hold her pressure."

The First Lieutenant nodded and passed on. What a grand feeling to have these experienced ratings for the backbone of this ship! So little was known yet. No one knew how the boat and its human material would stand up to wartime conditions.

He peered through the spyhole of the safety door to the reactor compartment. It was empty, so he passed through into the silent world of the nuclear power unit.

"How goes it, Chief?"

Chief E.R.A. Potts was wiping his hands on a bundle of cotton waste. He was a small man, dark haired and with beetling eyebrows. His lips pursed when he concentrated, and this gave him a peculiarly innocent air. He had an acid sense of humour, and his department jumped to it when they heard him coming.

"Fine, sir. There's nothing to do, compared with the old *Rugged*."

The First Lieutenant smiled. Funny how they all kept referring to the little *Rugged* of the Mediterranean days.

"Ready for the trim dive, Chief?"

"All ready, sir. I was just going to report to the Engineer Officer. He's down in the Hell-pit," and the Chief E.R.A. pointed downwards to where the reactor was housed, an enormous hunk of machinery shielded by thick slabs of lead. Spotlessly white, the yards of heavy piping writhed about the atomic reactor, eventually disappearing through the bulkhead and into the Turbine and Motor Rooms. Outside the after-end of the compartment was a vast panel and here sat the watchkeeper and his mate, intently watching the countless gauges and dials. Lieutenant Craig, the Engineer Officer, was inspecting the reactor at the moment. He looked up and waved at Benson. There was so little noise that he barely raised his voice to report that the Engine Room department was ready.

Benson still viewed the reactor with awe and he could never shake off the feeling that in the centre of that huge lump of lead there exploded a tiny fragment with enough power to obliterate hundreds of thousands of human beings; he shuddered as he imagined the consequences of the reactor running wild. There was something terrifying in the silent power of the reactor. It seemed incredible that it could drive these turbines and motors with such power for so long a period. Threading his way along the raised plating, he climbed along the catwalk until he reached the bulkhead of the Turbine and Motor Rooms. In here were the great pulsating power units which were more like the monsters he understood.

"All right, Brock?"

Benson addressed the Electrical Officer, Lieutenant Geoffrey Brocklebank, who had transferred to the electrical branch. This officer had been Sinclair's Third Hand in the Med and the Captain had especially asked him to join him in this new class of nuclears. Peter had been pleased, because as Third Hand of the first *Rugged* the chap had proved himself.

"All set, Number One. Leading Seaman Flint's on the switchboard."

Flint rose from his chair and grinned shyly. He still couldn't realise that he was in charge of such a vital piece of equipment. Gone were the enormous butt straps and the heavy switchgear of the conventional submarine's Motor Room. Instead, batteries of ammeters were arranged in rows, neat push-buttons doing substitute for the old long-handled switches with their enormous copper jaws. It was silent aft here. The purr of the shaft and the slip-slap of the wake overhead was all that could be heard.

Brocklebank saluted and Benson slowly made his way for'd. He was thoughtful because the trim dive was his responsibility. He had not trimmed her yet for a long war patrol and he was apprehensive of the result. He reached the Control Room below the fin and picked up the mike.

"Captain, sir?"

The speaker hummed for a second and then the voice of the man he knew so well crackled from the deckhead.

"Captain speaking."

"Number One here, sir. Ready for the Trim Dive."

"Thank you. We're approaching our diving position now. Tell the P.O. Tel. to clear the diving signal, Time of Origin, 0510."

"Aye, aye, sir."

"And Number One?"

"Sir?"

"Go to Diving Stations."

"Aye, aye, sir."

Benson flicked over the switch on the communication system and the speakers crackled throughout the ship.

"Diving stations!"

The First Lieutenant felt his heart quicken while the hands tumbled aft. He had almost forgotten what it was like to be on war patrol again, far from home and no one's particular chum!

He heard the telegraph clanging from aft and then he felt the way come off her. There was a rustle on the ladder and then Goddard, the Leading Signalman, tumbled down. He grinned at the Outside E.R.A. as he went for'd. Saunders was at the panel, waiting to open the vents.

There was silence. In the Control Room all eyes were turned upwards towards the Captain as he clambered down the ladder. "Take her down to periscope depth," he ordered.

The Commanding Officer's cabin was immediately below the fin. In here, at seven o'clock that same morning, as soon as the Trim Dive was successfully completed, the Captain assembled all his officers not on watch. The new Third Hand, Sub-Lieutenant Harold Spink, remained on watch in the Control Room and he was killing himself with impatience to discover their destination. *Rugged* was at periscope depth now, but Spink could see little future in their course which was still north-east.

"I've opened the sealed orders," Peter was saying. "I think I have a pretty clear idea of what's required of us. It's as I hoped, the real McCoy this time."

His officers sat round the small table expectantly, each with his own thoughts. Wish the Old Man would get on with it!

"These are our orders," the Captain began, and he read from the paper before him. "'One: To proceed dived with all despatch to the Caribbean area. Two: To carry out patrols between latitudes 21 degrees North and 10 degrees North and between longitudes 55 and 78 degrees West, and within thirty miles of all land.'"

"Phew!" Benson interrupted, "that should give us enough scope!"

Peter Sinclair paused and then continued quietly:

"'To sink all ships and submarines at sea which are on course for British territory. All, repeat all, friendly shipping has been warned off the area and an announcement is being made at this moment to this effect by the United Nations. For prestige reasons, the Totalitarian States have agreed to this U.N.O. action: they state that no ships of theirs could possibly be running arms and troops into the West Indian Federation.

"'It is reported, however, that submarines are operating in the area and are landing agents, troops and arms. Based on

Cuba, Santo Domingo and Puerto Rico, the submarines are to be destroyed if located within British territorial waters.

"'Three: All air cover has been withdrawn.

"'Four: H.M. Nuclear Submarine *Rugged* will be the only, repeat only, U.N.O. warship in the area.

"'Five: To carry out a full reconnaissance of the area.

"'*Note.* It is emphasised that should the submarine be sunk or captured, Their Lordships will be unable to acknowledge responsibility, nor will Her Majesty's Government be able to admit knowledge of the operation. Secrecy is therefore vital and at no time should the submarine be sighted.'"

Peter looked up at his officers. The real meaning of war had struck home. It wasn't the fun and the glory that young men were misled into believing. It was just hell, sheer, unmitigated hell, punctuated by spells of boredom, and they were beginning to realise it. Their smiles had vanished.

"I'm now turning about and will set course for the Windward Passage. It's about a thousand miles and we shall remain dived throughout the patrol. You can take it that we are now on war patrol. To put it bluntly, that means *it's either us or the enemy*."

The First Lieutenant passed a hand over his sleek, black hair. "It's as well I stocked right up, sir. This job might last months."

"Yes, Number One. I shall be exercising action conditions on the run down to our billet and at four o'clock on Monday morning we shall be entering our patrol area. I intend to patrol in the Windward Passage to watch the flow of shipping. Any submarine from Santiago will have to pass through that nodal point, if bound for Jamaica or the West Indies."

"Is that where they're operating from, sir?"

"Yes, and Puerto Rico. But they're supposed to prefer Cuba, and I can't say I blame 'em! Any questions?"

"What about communications, sir?" Brocklebank asked. "Normal war routine and W/T silence?"

"Yes. Anything else…? Go to patrol routine, then, First Lieutenant. I'll talk to the ship's company when they've finished breakfast. Alter course for the Windward Passage, Pilot. Full speed."

Peter was left alone with his thoughts. He'd drive them hard for the next two days, exercising every conceivable emergency until they were efficient. Their existence depended upon their skill, and what was worse so did the fate of countless people. He changed into his patrol rig of khaki shirt, shorts, sandals, and his favourite cap, a greasy relic of the past, a battered and a revered 'joss' object. He always wore it, once on patrol, though it had seen better, but not prouder days. He slid through the narrow door and clambered down into the Control Room. He picked up the speaker and throughout the boat men stopped what they were doing when they heard the voice they had come to know so well.

"This is the Captain speaking," he began. "I've got some good news for you…"

It was customary for the First Lieutenant to take the first half of the morning watch, from midnight to two, so it was Benson who first sighted Inagua early on the Monday morning of April 15th. They had left the Caicos Islands astern some time ago and now they were beginning to worry about their position. Ian Taggart sighed with relief.

"I'll tell the Captain, Number One," the sandy-haired Scot volunteered. "From my fix, I think we should alter up to the westward a bit."

And so at dawn on Monday, Peter saw through his periscope the eastern extremity of Cuba, fine on the starboard bow. Grey, hot and sticky, a foul-looking place. Why anyone should want the darned island he couldn't think. The Commies were welcome to it. And then his heart leapt.

In the circle of the periscope lens there appeared three cross-trees, white crosses he had seen before so often. They could belong to warships and his heart began racing. At last, perhaps...?

"Diving Stations!"

The battle cry of the submariners rang through the boat. Men streamed to their stations, relieving those on watch, so that they could man their positions in the remoter parts of the submarine.

"Bearing THAT! One destroyer... Bearing THAT! Another destroyer... THAT! Another... Down periscope."

The steel tube slid down into the well, gleaming and hissing like some evil serpent. The Captain turned to his new Third Hand, an inane young man and a natural comedian in his lighter moments. Nothing went right for him. Sub-Lieutenant Harry Spink would go far, but in which direction no one yet dared hazard a guess.

"There are five destroyers, Sub, and I am ten degrees on the starboard bow of the leader. Speed, twelve knots: by their bow waves, I shouldn't think they're doing much more. What's the range?"

The angular young man twiddled the knobs on the instrument which was still affectionately known as the Fruit Machine, though it was hardly recognisable from its famous forebears.

"Three thousand yards, sir. Course for a sixty track, o-three-two."

"Up periscope. Anything on the Asdic yet?"

The question was thrown at the H.S.D., Petty Officer David Elliott, a dependable man. He had to be. Crouched up now in his cramped Asdic cabinet, he listened carefully for enemy Asdic transmissions and propeller noises.

"Faint H.E., Green one-five, sir."

"Any transmissions?"

"No, sir, can't pick up anything yet, but I'll try another frequency… Hullo, what's this?" The dark-haired man clamped the earphones tighter to his head.

And then, before they realised it, they could hear the enemy Asdic transmissions ticking against their pressure hull. *Like the noise you make when you gently flick your finger and thumb together*, thought Peter. *It's strange to hear it again. These can't be Cuban-manned ships. By their lines, there's not much doubt where they come from*, and he snapped shut the handles of the periscope.

"Port ten, steer two-one-o," Peter said quietly. "Silent routine."

The First Lieutenant repeated the order and then only the faint whine of fans and telemotor machinery could be heard throughout the boat.

"Course, sir, two-one-o," the helmsman reported as he swung the steering wheel. A grubby neckerchief was round his neck and this caught the sweat that was running down his bare back.

"This should give them the slip, Number One. I'm stern-on to them now. Up periscope."

The Outside E.R.A. swung off on the periscope lever and the instrument, the Captain's 'eye', raced upwards. Peter grabbed the handles as it swept by. He bored his eyes into the foam eyepiece; the glass broke surface; the light streamed into the lens, blurred and streaky for an instant while the hot sun evaporated the moisture from the sloping face. Then it suddenly cleared, bringing the object sharply into focus.

"Bearing THAT... Destroyer, I'm fifteen degrees on her starboard bow, range THAT."

He pulled away from the eyepiece and the periscope slid downwards. He felt worried.

"I believe they're turning towards, Number One. You know what that means."

"They're in contact, sir."

"Asdic transmissions in contact, sir, Green one-two-o. Destroyer H.E. on same bearing, increasing," Elliott said quietly from his corner. His eyes met his Captain's. This was a bit sudden — they hadn't got their first wind yet.

"Up periscope."

Peter swept round quickly, first in low power for aircraft, and then in high power. He glanced at the advancing destroyers. The nearest was pointing straight towards, and already her superstructure had climbed above the horizon. There was no nonsense about her: she was dazzle-painted in grey and green and it was difficult to estimate her angle-on-the-bow. His heart raced as he saw her two consorts opening out at full speed on either side of her. White bow waves creamed at their sterns and a mountain of water built up and foamed at their sterns, while a long hollow of boot-topping showed in between. They were powerful-looking ships and obviously well drilled. Peter disliked the look of the mortar barrels trained over the side. He thought he saw the rotating blades of a helicopter whirling in the sun as it warmed up on the quarterdeck of the left-hand ship.

"Down periscope. Range?"

The tick-ticking was everywhere now, insinuating and remorseless. It crept into your brain, and nowhere could you escape it … tick-tick … tick … tick … tick … *They've got us taped all right*, thought Peter.

"Stand by one, two, three, and four tubes," Peter rapped, his mind made up. "Depth setting, twelve feet. Let's see if this will cool their ardour. Target ship, centre destroyer!"

The Captain flicked his thumb and middle finger and the attack periscope flashed upwards, a sliver of steel that barely rippled the surface. He spun round in a quick aircraft sweep: the helicopter was airborne now, only a couple of hundred yards away.

"Bearing THAT … range THAT… Down periscope."

He was using the stick carefully now, but mercifully the morning breeze was causing a slight flurry on the surface.

"I'm ten degrees on her port bow. She's increasing speed — give her eighteen knots. Starboard fifteen, half ahead."

The Sub was feeding the information into the Fruit Machine with one hand while taking a message down the phone from the Tube Space with the other. The mauve lights of the Torpedo Ready lamp-box were flickering above his head.

"Transmission interval decreased, sir," Elliott reported. "This gives a range of eight hundred yards."

Peter nodded. The Asdic transmissions could be heard all round them.

"Ship's head?"

"Two-six-five, sir."

"Shut off from depth-charge attack, Number One. I'll run under to see if that will shake them off."

"Aye, aye, sir," said Benson quietly, and he repeated the order on the broadcasting system. The massive doors between the bulkheads began to swing shut. The clips snapped over the black ferrules and they were alone in their compartment.

"All tubes ready, sir."

"Stand by!"

The periscope swished upwards.

"Stand by, sir," said the Sub, a note of excitement creeping into his voice at this, his first attack.

"H.E. increasing, sir."

Peter grasped the periscope handles as the tube slid by. He glued his eyes into the foam eyepiece. The dark blue of the water quickly changed to a turquoise green. Then he could see the underside of the surface, mottled and mazy with the light which was diffusing through the film of unreality that separated the two worlds of air and water.

The lens broke surface and a ray of light streamed into the irises of his eyes. For an eternity the image was blurred while the water drained from the sloping lens. In reality hardly a second had elapsed, but Peter could feel his heart hammering. He felt sick and he gripped the handles for reassurance. In a few seconds, before they'd even started their operation, the enemy had won and were about to blast them into fragments. *They seemed to be expecting him.* The thought flashed through his mind, and then the lens cleared.

"THAT... FIRE ONE!" He slammed the periscope handles shut. "Fire by time interval, Emergency Change of Depth, two hundred feet, full speed ahead! Ease the wheel, steer north!"

The orders streamed from his lips, clearly and decisively. Stoker Petty Officer Hicks, who was reading off the bearing ring, saw the old light of battle flickering again in his Captain's eyes and he realised that this must be a touch-and-go affair. He moved over to the telegraph and stood by the young seaman who was the operator. His name was Thatcher, and he'd not been long in The Trade.

"Flood Q!" the First Lieutenant snapped.

The Outside E.R.A. yanked at the red-handled switch. There was a dull boom as tons of water hurtled into the emergency diving tank. Then she started on her way down, the pointers trembling in the gauges.

"Keep her stern down, for God's sake, Number One. There's a helicopter over the top of us," Peter murmured.

It was some years since he'd carried out an attack under wartime conditions, and he was surprised how little he'd forgotten. But he had been unprepared for the quick retaliation of the enemy. They had caught him unprepared mentally, and now *Rugged* was about to pay the price. He groaned inwardly and instinctively glanced at the curved deckhead above him. The destroyers must be racing in for the kill now. He cocked his head to hear the better.

"Five hundred yards, sir," the H.S.D. shouted above the roar of 'Q'. His black head crouched low over the illuminated dial, but now he had removed the earphones. He didn't want to lose his eardrums when the patterns exploded. Elliott might still be on exercises in Weymouth Bay for all the notice he was taking of events.

Peter clenched his teeth. The mortars must be firing now and he could see the trajectory of the projectiles in his mind as they curved high into the air to come plummeting downwards over the submarine's line of advance. No, he'd never forget his last periscope sighting.

The tips of a red helicopter's revolving blades were what he registered first. He remembered it seeming strange that he couldn't hear the typical flutter which the blades made and he wondered whether the pilot could see *Rugged*'s stick. The helicopter had cocked up its tail suddenly and had come swooping towards him. From its belly there streamed a long wire with a round drum at the end swinging in a wide parabola.

He just had time to glance at the nearest destroyer. She seemed within a cable and he was fine on her port bow. The flare of her fo'c'sle showed prominently and she had a bone in her teeth as she lunged towards them. A bunch of seamen was huddled on the port side and they were pointing excitedly. They were a comical sight as they supported each other, afraid of falling over the side as she bucked, now that her guardrails were slipped for action stations. The barrels of her twin for'd mounting pointed wickedly over her bow, while from her funnel a wisp of blue haze came in guffs as the engine rooms gave full power for the attack. He remembered seeing with surprise the red bunting streaming at the yardarms, and then he noticed, just abaft the bridge, the whisker aerials bending in the wind. They must be manoeuvring on short wave.

Before their minds had assimilated how great the noise had grown, a terrifying racket swamped them. Then, as the beat of propellers started pounding in their ears, there was a shattering explosion. Even at a hundred and fifty feet, the pressure was so colossal that the curved sides of the submarine sprang inwards like a concertina with terrifying suddenness. There was a tinkling of water noises, then a strange pattering, like raindrops on a tin roof. Silence followed. Their first torpedo had found its target.

"Number One Torpedo fired, sir!" Sub-Lieutenant Harold Spink reported nonchalantly.

There was a gale of laughter around the Control Room. The Subbie certainly lived up to expectations. Peter rounded on him, anger bled from him by the innocence of the Idiot Boy.

"You buffoon, Sub!"

A cheer echoed round the Control Room and Hicks chalked up a tick in red chalk above the panel.

"Our first sinking," he muttered.

"H.E. increasing, Red one-hundred, sir."

The Control Room crew turned on Elliott almost with distaste. Peter felt his stomach sinking at the H.S.D.'s words. He'd forgotten the other hunters. They'd give *Rugged* little mercy now.

"Full ahead," he snapped. "Let's see if they can keep up."

He moved quickly to the chart table.

"Where are we, Pilot?" he asked. "Plenty of water?"

Taggart stabbed the chart with his finger. "Here, sir; two miles, one-eight-six, Cabo Maysi. There's no bottom charted here. We're just about over Kidd's Deep."

Peter returned to his vantage point between the periscopes.

"We're in luck. According to Sailing Directions this is one of the deepest holes in the world. Eight hundred feet. Take her down quickly, Number One."

"Aye, aye, sir." There was a glint of amusement in Benson's eyes. Both the Coxswain and he enjoyed this. He tapped the Coxswain's shoulder.

"Eight hundred feet, Cox'n."

The grizzled veteran twisted the control-bar of the afterplanes and the sensitive reactions of the men in the Control Room immediately felt her take on a bow-down angle. They watched the bubble glide aft in the inclinometers, and then she was swooping downwards under perfect control.

"Shut main ballast Kingstons. Shut shallow-water diving gauges," the First Lieutenant ordered quietly.

The Captain had to raise his voice above the clatter of water noises: "Open main vents!"

Rugged trembled from the power and torque of her huge propeller as she worked up to full speed.

"H.E. increasing, sir. Destroyer running in to attack."

Above their own water noises, they could hear the hunters thundering over them, the beat of their propellers pounding, pounding, pounding… Then the attacking destroyer was overhead. Peter glanced at Elliott. The man had removed his earphones and was watching his pointers.

Peter was holding on to the ladder. The boat was at a steep angle, about twenty degrees bow-down, he thought, and was going down fast. It was an emergency change of depth, an evolution that they often exercised. She was behaving beautifully, like a glider in the hands of a sensitive pilot. Number One had complete control, and the Cox'n was taking off the angle when the first pattern exploded. *Rugged* was doing all of twenty-five knots when it struck. She lurched from the blow, there was a shattering crash, and a peculiar hissing. Men gasped as the wind was knocked from them and then came sudden darkness.

A moment of fear, of clutching, overwhelming panic. Men struggled to regain their feet, slipped, and grabbed at anything to haul themselves upright. Then the emergency lighting flickered on. The pale lighting cast weird shadows about the Control Room to betray the animal fear that clutched each man. Darkness concealed the weaknesses but now truth was stripped bare.

"After-planes jammed hard-a-dive, sir!"

There was a note of urgency in the Coxswain's voice. Already the boat was diving more steeply, the bubble creeping up the curved inclinometer tube. Men were sliding down the sloping corticene and gear was breaking loose.

"Stop main motor! Emergency astern, after-planes in hand!"

Peter had recognised instinctively that this was an emergency: he must grapple with it before it got out of hand. The pointers on the gauges were racing round the dials now and had already passed the thousand feet mark. The red line of the safe diving depth had just been crossed. After this no one knew when she would collapse from the pressures…

The noise of the destroyer decreased as she drew down the starboard side, but this went unheeded in the confusion inside the submarine that was hurtling to its own destruction.

"Fore-planes hard-a-rise," the First Lieutenant snapped, and he felt all eyes boring into his back as he wrestled for control. A low rumble as her screws threshed astern and then there was sudden quiet, an ominous, dreadful silence. Peter turned towards the telegraph operator, but he was correct: the indicators showed Emergency Astern. If the main motor fuses had blown…

The phone from the Motor Room shrilled and the young seaman, the white-faced Thatcher, yanked the instrument from its rest. "Control Room?" he shouted.

He turned to face his Captain; his lips worked but no sound came. He swallowed, then he said: "Main motor fuses blown, sir. They're doing all they can to replace them."

In their haste to go astern and to give the motors full power for the emergency, the Motor Room crew had allowed the surge of current to become too great. They must be having a thin time of it in there, surrounded by choking fumes as they worked in the dark to replace the enormous fuses.

The Captain turned towards the gauges. Twelve hundred and thirty feet and still going down! He had one last chance and that was to blow Main Ballast. He had left this for the last resort because the gobs of air would burst on the surface as enormous, tell-tale bubbles.

"Shut main vents," he ordered calmly.

The Outside E.R.A.'s hands snaked over the panel as he flicked the switches and then, from far away, came the dull thunks of the vents.

"All main vents checked shut, sir."

The First Lieutenant's eyes met his Captain's and each knew that this was their last chance — twelve hundred and eighty feet, yet she was still holding! They both thrust the nightmare of the impending catastrophe from their imaginations. The main lighting flashed on as the after-ends phone screamed.

"Water coming in through the stern gland, sir!" Thatcher yelled, a note of hysteria creeping into his voice.

Here it comes, Peter thought as he thrust his hands into his pockets. *This is it…*

"Blow one Main Ballast. Give her all you've got, Saunders."

The Outside E.R.A., the Cornishman from Mullion, nodded at his Captain. He spun the T-shaped valve. Air screamed along the high-pressure line, whining and singing. They could do nothing now but wait.

The gauge showed thirteen hundred feet but the bows must be a hundred feet deeper. Each man was listening to catch the first sounds of breaking up, the scrunching of buckling metal, the roar of engulfing water…

The for'd phone shrilled and the Sub's hand shot out for it. At the same moment Elliott spoke from his Asdic set.

"Loud H.E. Red one-two-o, sir. Running in to attack."

"Water coming in through the fore-hatch, sir," the Sub said quietly, his face a mask but with frightened eyes.

They all heard the mortars striking the surface — snik! — snik! — snik, snik, snik! and each man waited in his own private hell. Peter watched the deckhead, Benson the gauges. Breathing stopped while they waited for the tumbling projectiles, swinging down through the depths. They exploded on impact, so only one hit was needed. If the mortars did not find you, they'd explode at a predetermined depth…

Then Peter felt the strain coming off his arms. The bows were lifting! Only thirty degrees bow-down now, and the way coming off her slowly; eight knots only now by the log. They had a chance…

"Stop blowing!"

A shock hit them then with a reverberating roar that hurt their eardrums. They reeled from the blow that struck blindly from above, a mortal, cruel onslaught that paralysed them with its devastating power. The deck jumped under them. The sides of the boat sprang inwards. The gauge pointers started to move again as the main lighting flickered out. In the darkness, Peter knew that this was the end — she could take no more. The depths would snatch her now. The emergency lights flicked on, the bows fell away again and she continued her downward plunge.

"Blow all main ballast!" Peter yelled. "Keep blowing!"

And in the semi-darkness they watched the futile efforts of Saunders as he wrestled with the 'blows'. She was away now, out of control, spiralling downwards like a falling leaf into the deeps. Peter shut his eyes. He could hear nothing but the pounding of his heart…

Then they realised gradually that the angle was lessening, that she was listing to port — they could feel it under their feet! Peter glanced at the gauge — she wasn't falling any more. She was stationary at fourteen hundred and twenty feet: he must be dreaming! He shook his head but then there was a dull screeching noise, and she seemed to halt in her wild descent. The heavy body of the Second Coxswain fell off his stool. The boat had struck something.

"Stop blowing!" he gasped.

The shriek of air ceased. There was silence then, complete, total, when time stood still… In the semi-darkness Peter glimpsed the extent of the shambles: the telegraphs were still at Emergency Astern, the First Lieutenant was on his knees. Thatcher was lying full length on his stomach and was clinging to a valve spindle by his hands; the helmsman was squeezed against the wheel and was trying to extricate himself; Taggart was struggling upright to the chart table. Spink was sitting in a fire-bucket, his feet higher than his head.

"Stop main motors! All compartments make your reports."

What had happened? What had arrested their plunge to destruction? The Main Ballast tanks were full of air. She must have full buoyancy, but why was she not swooping upwards? Instead, she was lying immobile at an absurd angle — eighteen degrees bow-down and with a seven degrees list to port…

"We must have landed on a submarine mountaintop, Number One," Peter said quietly. "Now who doesn't believe in miracles?" He grinned as he looked at his men: they'd had the stuffing knocked out of them all right.

"Come on, Number One, let's get on with it. Clear up the mess and let's show the devils up top who's boss. Get cracking!"

Then the reports came in:

Water trickling in through the stern gland…

"Was it serious?"

No, sir, nothing that the pumps couldn't cope with.

But the pumps won't operate at this depth… Well, they'd have to watch the bilges, that's all.

They'd let the Control Room know when the level got dangerous.

Peter was worried by the nonchalance of his ship's company. In this 'nuclear', with her secondary batteries, had they forgotten about chlorine gas.

"For'd all right?"

Not too bad, considering. Bit of bother in the pump space, but only a small trickle coming in through the valve box. Didn't advise operating the valves though, at this depth.

"Engine Room?"

Oh yes, the Engine Room Department was all right as usual. No, there was nothing they wanted, thank you; the reactor seemed quite happy; but how was it in the Control Room? Not too bad, considering...

Peter smiled grimly. Well, things could be worse.

"H.E., Green one-one-o, sir. Passing down the starboard side," said Elliott. Peter heard a groan from Thatcher and his own stomach heaved with nausea. They held their breath...

In the silence they heard the whistlings and chucklings of the water noises as the hunter sniffed about overhead for the final coup de grâce.

"Absolute silence from everyone, Number One."

The enemy had lost them temporarily. If they pinpointed *Rugged* now, her fate was sealed. She was a sitting target, stuck firmly in the Caribbean mud and at some incredible depth.

As they waited, each man pushed the workings of his imagination into his subconscious... The whisper above them faded slowly, slowly...

There was a clang against the pressure hull, and the reverberations from the shock waves echoed through the deeps.

"H.E. stopped, sir. Last bearing on Red one-six-o and Green one-seven-o."

"Thank you, Elliott. Carry on with an all-round listening watch."

Saunders was staring at his Captain. When he caught his eye, he tapped the high-pressure gauge.

"Not much H.P. air left, sir."

Peter paused involuntarily.

"How much?"

"Not enough for one long 'guff', sir."

Peter strolled around the Control Room. He thrust his hands into his pockets and watched the men cleaning up the mess. *Rugged* was in a spot. Stuck in the mud at her diving limit, hunted overhead, she'd better lie doggo. At least no water was coming in, she had plenty of amps and the reactor was undamaged. But they were stuck fast and there was no air for blowing. They were in a predicament and he could see no way out.

The after-ends phone light was blipping. Peter was relieved to see young Thatcher's face relax as he took the message — no worse news, anyhow.

"Ready to try main motors, sir. Fuses replaced."

"Very good. Tell them they'll have to wait until the heat's off. I'll be speaking to the ship's company as soon as it's safe to do so."

And an hour later, as the search for them drew further to the westward, Peter decided to break the news to his men. He'd had time to think and he'd come to a decision. But while the enemy were around, he dared attempt nothing. They had been saved by this uncharted pinnacle, and Providence was not likely to give them a second chance. He picked up the mike.

"Captain speaking," he began. "The heat has now decreased sufficiently for us to open up from depth-charging. But I'm taking no risks, and in case the enemy is lying stopped and is listening for us on the surface, I'll wait till dark before trying to free ourselves.

"We are well and truly stuck, and we'll need every pound of air to free us. We've used nearly all the H.P. air we have, and there's not enough in the bottles to finish blowing main ballast.

I propose to run the compressors on the air we are breathing in order to top up the bottles. I don't know what effect it will have on our breathing or whether our lungs will collapse, but I can think of no alternative. We'll go to Diving Stations at nine o'clock when we'll start running the compressors.

"You will all realise the seriousness of our position. The less air we use, the better our chances. So until further orders, get your heads down, keep silence and don't eat. The boat is in good fettle, there is no increase in radioactivity, and we're not downhearted. All I want to do, personally, is to return the compliment to our friends up top."

Peter replaced the mike with a sinking feeling in his stomach. He smiled at Number One and asked for a chair to be brought into the Control Room. Then he sat down between the periscopes to listen to Elliott's routine reports. The enemy seemed to be drawing steadily away.

"Probably think they've got us taped, sir," Elliott smiled.

"What a ridiculous idea, sir," Taggart broke in. "We're not even warmed up yet. But it's amazing how time flies under these conditions, isn't it?"

It was nearly four o'clock.

"Diving stations!"

No one had slept much, and they welcomed the summons. It was best to get on with it, best to know the worst. If they couldn't shake free… well, they'd have to face that ordeal later.

"All-round sweep completed, sir. Nothing to report."

Elliott was almost nodding at his set. He'd been closed up for fifteen hours and was exhausted.

"Start the compressors."

The Captain snapped out the order. He'd been turning the problem over in his mind. There was no alternative.

The vibration of the compressors rumbled through the boat. If there was anyone up top now, this noise would betray them. They waited, watching Elliott. He turned towards the Captain and shook his head. "Nothing to report." He smiled. A sigh rustled through the Control Room.

The hammering of the compressors continued for seven minutes before the first effects on their breathing was felt. Then they realised gradually that although breathing out was astonishingly easy, inhaling was becoming an effort.

All eyes in the Control Room watched the H.P. air pressure gauge. The needle hardly moved. A faint trembling, that was all. Peter's eyes ached as he stared at it. He turned away, a ridiculous superstition swamping him that if he watched, nothing would happen. He heard the First Lieutenant speaking next to him.

"The Coxswain wonders whether we could do a bit of praying, sir?"

Peter nodded. Chief Petty Officer Withers knew what was what. The compressor would have to stop in a few minutes, for men were gasping already.

"It's moving now, sir."

The Outside E.R.A. was tapping the gauge, and he looked hard at his Captain. "There's just enough for one good blow, sir."

"Stop the compressors. Check main vents shut."

The ensuing silence was unnerving. Each man knew that they stood poised on the brink: if this last puff didn't free her, they were doomed to slow suffocation…

"Slow astern…"

The order was passed by phone, then the main motor purred into life. They watched the depth gauges. But there was no sign of movement, even after a full minute's running.

"Half astern."

Peter bit his lips. He'd keep the air until he'd tried everything. He let her drive for over two minutes, but even with her enormous propeller she refused to budge. "Stop main motor."

He reached up for the mike.

"Captain speaking. The Coxswain has suggested that this is a moment for prayer. In a moment I shall be going full astern and I'll be using the last of our high pressure air for blowing Main Ballast. We shall need God's help also." The speakers clicked as he snapped off the switch.

The boat was very quiet. This was not a moment for self-consciousness and most men bowed their heads. Peter closed his eyes. Then he turned slowly towards the young man on the phone.

"Full astern," he ordered. "Stand by to blow Main Ballast."

Saunders stood feet astride by his panel. He was watching the H.P. air gauge, his arms outstretched, one hand clasping the wheel spanner, the other the handwheel of the valve. He was waiting…

Peter felt the revs building up, the boat starting to tremble from the sudden surge of astern power. There was a rasping noise right aft and the boat quivered. The noise grew louder and increased to a deafening crescendo like a train shooting a tunnel. Peter was watching the depth gauge for a sign … watching, just for a flicker… One minute … one and a half … but now the roar was overwhelming and nothing made sense any more. She hadn't budged.

The Captain turned towards the panel: "Blow Main Ballast!"

CHAPTER 4

Overdue

The Commodore was looking out over the turquoise sea. It was too grand a morning to stay bottled up at this confounded conference. Golf at the Mid-Ocean was more the order of the day. The scarlets and blues of his shrubs danced in the wind against the dark green of the cypresses, while, down below, the Cove was flecked by white horses. The Commodore could guess what each officer was going to say even before he opened the conference, but they would get a shock today. Some of his staff might get sent to sea yet, and he smiled wickedly to himself as he thought of the predicament they would find themselves in. He wondered how that nuclear was getting on. *Rugged*, wasn't she? That young fellow Sinclair seemed to know what he was doing, but the Commodore, for one, had no taste for three months in that sardine tin. He could hear his snotty-nosed Flag-Lieutenant coughing tactfully behind him. God! How he wished he was like Sinclair and twenty-five years younger. He'd show them, as that young man in the Caribbean was doing at the moment…

"Good morning, gentlemen. Let's get on with the business."

The old sea dog waved his hands impatiently for them to be seated. From the Old Man's temper this morning something must have gone wrong and the atmosphere was tense with expectation. The Secretariat and U.N.O. officers were looking smug, and were infuriating the officers of the Royal Navy because obviously they had learnt of the news already.

"This is an up-to-date situation report, gentlemen. I have summoned you here because things have come to a head in the Caribbean. We have just received reports from our agents that a full-scale uprising and takeover bid is scheduled to take place in the near future."

The Commodore paused for effect and there was a murmur round the table. But most of his audience had been expecting this for months; what they were not expecting, however, was the news that followed.

"But, for once we have been ordered to do something about it." The Old Man's eyes flashed as he pounded the table. "By God, instead of sitting around on our backsides and watching the Commies trump all the tricks, we're actually ordered, *ordered*, gentlemen, to take remedial action."

His audience had risen to their feet and something extraordinary took place in that staid and sombre room. Months of planning and years of pent-up frustration were released in the cheer that echoed round the room. The Commodore was grim and, when he made them sit down, his eyes glittered.

"You must all realise the background to this situation. More and more of the local police have defected and there are reports that even some of the less-well-to-do planters have gone over to the enemy."

"But how, sir, do the enemy have such a hold over the population of these scattered islands?" asked a Commander in the Secretariat Branch. "After all, the West Indies are a Federation."

"It seems that there is a fanatical leader," the Commodore continued, "called the Serpent King. He has an incredible hold over the natives. There is an initiation ceremony and, once a man has been involved in this, his whole family is blackmailed to join the Party. This Serpent King uses the same sort of foul juju as the Mau Mau did in Kenya way back in the fifties. He uses a replica of the fer-de-lance, the West Indian snake, as a sort of fetish, and around this a nightmare existence has been fostered. Son informs against father, daughter against mother — the usual totalitarian horror, I'm afraid.."

The Commodore paused, glowered at the water carafe, and continued: "The failure of the efforts of U.N.I.C.E.F. makes things worse. The starvation that has followed in the path of unrest has been exploited to the full by the Communists. The wretched natives are in search of succour from U.N.I.C.E.F.'s supplies which arrive in the islands, but the corruption of the middle classes snatches the food from under the very noses of the poor. They are forced to pay absurd prices if they want the food. With their usual hypocrisy, the Commies are holding up their hands in righteous indignation. U.N.I.C.E.F. is being ridiculed, so the West Indian turns his back in scorn upon our efforts to help. A hungry man does not sit down on his backside, gentlemen, and watch his children die from starvation. In the last resort, he revolts: riots are breaking out all over the islands."

"Any idea of the final date of rebellion, sir?" the Signals Officer asked.

"None so far, but we know it's imminent."

"What can we do about it, sir, if local opinion is against us, and is entirely won over by this serpent stuff?"

There was a pause while all eyes watched the brisk figure of the Commodore. He had turned his back and was gazing out of the windows. *How secure everything looked from here*, he thought, *but who knows, perhaps the disease will spread even to these delightful islands before very long. The Wind of Change…*

"Well, there's one thing we can do," he mused, "and that is to discover just what is going on in the islands, and upon whom we can count for loyalty."

There was a knock on the door and the Chief Yeoman of Signals entered. The Commodore did not notice him as he crept silently round to the Flag-Lieutenant. This young man glanced at the pink slip of paper and then his eyebrows moved imperceptibly above his aristocratic nose. He nodded at the Yeoman who withdrew. The monotone of the Commodore's address was interrupted by a discreet cough from his Flag-Lieutenant.

"Immediate signal, sir."

"Don't interrupt, James," the Commodore snorted, "can't you see I'm busy? Read it."

Flags cleared his throat.

"Well, for God's sake, what is it?" the Old Man snorted.

"*Rugged*'s overdue, sir."

CHAPTER 5

Red Tooth, Red Claw

"Blow Main Ballast!"

The order flickered through the boat, from mouth to mouth. In the silence they heard the scream of the air in the high-pressure line. The sound was high-pitched, nearly supersonic, but then, as the air ran out, the noise gradually decreased until, with the last few pounds, it died away completely. The boat shuddered from the frenzied churnings of her propeller, and the hull whipped.

Peter's eyes were everywhere: on the depth gauge, the bubbles, the H.P. air gauge, the telegraph. As the scream in the airline died away, so did hope. *I'll hold on another half-minute,* he thought. *If we don't break free, it doesn't matter much if I've wasted the amps. Probably the best thing, for it'll help to cut short the agony…*

The noise in the airline had died away and Saunders was gazing in disbelief at the H.P. air gauge; he seemed in a trance, mesmerised by the stationary pointer that was now resting against the stops. He was panting from his exertions and his lungs hurt.

Peter glanced at his wristwatch — another three seconds — and he dragged his eyes from the gauge. He passed his hand over his face and then he shouted at the telegraphsman, Thatcher.

"Stop main motors."

The rumble died away, there were a few whistling water noises, and then there was silence. Their moment had come; there was no escaping the ordeal now.

"I'd like to speak to the ship's company, Number One. Get them into the Control Room, please."

The First Lieutenant slowly picked up the mike. His voice was steady when he spoke: "All hands in the Control Room, all hands in the Control Room."

They heard the shuffle of approaching men, and in the disturbance no one but the Outside E.R.A. felt the first tremor. His arms still remained outstretched on the panel and this must have acted as a shock-absorber. It was a second or two before he realised what was happening…

"We're moving, sir!" he yelled, brokenly. "The old girl's movin', sir, I'm zartin of it. She's movin'!" He turned towards his Captain. Unashamedly the Cornishman dashed away the tears with the back of his hand.

Peter stood astride, watching the depth gauge and bubble. He felt it then; a faint shudder, a tremor that quivered the length of the boat. As he watched, the bubble slid slowly along the yellow-green inclinometer. It came amidships then ran along until it steadied at five degrees bow-up.

"Full astern! Diving stations!"

She was breaking her bonds, free from the suffocating mud, and Peter wanted to yell exultantly. When the hands came aft, the shift of weight must have made the extra difference and she had broken free. He heard the hands rushing to their stations as *Rugged* started to bound from her uncharted pinnacle.

The next moment they were off their feet and slithering about the deck. The bubble had rushed up against the stops and she was now lurching to an incredible bow-up angle: *must be at least thirty degrees*, thought Peter, as he struggled to regain his feet. The pointer on the gauge was beginning to move now — they had already risen a hundred feet and the pointer was backing fast up the dial. Then a horrible fear crept into Peter's mind. Would the reactor, would the turbines be able to take much more of an angle? They'd never tried more than forty degrees on trials. But, dear God, what about the danger from chlorine!

"Open Number One Main Vent! Stop motor."

Peter's order rapped through the pandemonium, and he heard the *thunk!* of the vents opening, away in the bows. Streams of air must be bubbling to the surface now, boiling and bursting in great gouts, but what did that matter? Even if the enemy were waiting for them, they'd prefer to be mown down as they crawled out, to the death they had been facing three minutes earlier.

But Peter had to be careful. If he admitted too much water for'd, she'd sink by the bows again: there was no air left with which to blow main ballast now. And he wondered with amusement whether the after planes were in power yet? But it didn't matter. The Coxswain was huddled in a heap by the Asdic cabinet, squashed by the dead weight of the First Lieutenant, and on top of him, the sprawling figure of the Second Coxswain.

Thatcher had climbed up to swing the telegraph and now the propeller had stopped turning. Nothing could be heard now except loose gear crashing about and men's muffled oaths.

Eight hundred feet, seven hundred, six… She was flying upwards at a terrifying rate. The deck had become a sloping wall in front of him, and Peter found himself hanging on to the lip of the for'd periscope well. He was almost upright, so she couldn't be far from vertical. From the corner of his eye he glimpsed the gauge: two hundred feet, one hundred and fifty…

She'd shoot from the sea like an arrow and break her back as she flopped downwards. She couldn't stand the shock, and

Peter braced himself for the sickening lurch. One hundred feet … her bows must surely have broken surface by now and be rearing high into the night, and he shut his eyes as he waited for the smack of her fore-ends as she settled down again by the head.

The gauge remained at forty-two feet. She fell away slightly, but her hull remained seventy degrees bow-up. The gauge was steady at this depth, but it was impossible to work the ship.

"Number One?"

"Sir?"

"I'm going up the tower. Stand by to surface and send up the signalman."

"Aye, aye, sir. Stand by to surface!" yelled the First Lieutenant from the Control Room. "We'll soon have her straight, sir."

Peter managed to open the lower conning tower hatch, climbing the ladder was another matter. He lay on his back and the rungs ran horizontally above him. If he let go he would merely fall a couple of feet against the after side of the fin which was now directly beneath him. There was no light, for he couldn't find the switch at this ridiculous angle.

"Captain, sir?"

Goddard's voice came echoing up the tower.

"Yes?"

"Shall I go first to open the lid?"

This was normally the signalman's duty, the Captain hanging on to the man's legs to prevent him being blown over the side by the excess pressure from inside the submarine.

"No, it's all right, thanks. I don't know yet whether the upper lid's under water. We'll have to use the forehatch if it is. Are you ready?"

"Yes, sir."

"Hold on to my legs then."

When Peter felt the strong hands about his ankles, he removed the first clip.

"Depth?" he shouted into the gloom below him.

There was a pause. No one had heard him.

"Depth?" Goddard bellowed.

The First Lieutenant eventually struggled to the lower lid and shouted up the tower: "Twenty-eight feet and steady at that, sir."

She must be half out of the water!

"I'm opening up."

Peter took off the other clip, but it required all his strength to shove open the upper lid. The pressure inside the boat was less than atmospheric because he had run the compressors on the internal air. The lid burst open and his hands were nearly pulled from his wrists as the spring of the hatch and its inertia took charge. Then he felt the night air.

Not far below him the sea gurgled and swished about the hull, while far above him the mass of fore-deck loomed blackly against the sky. It took a moment for him to get his bearings, and then he felt the angle gently coming off her. Number One had regained control.

A few minutes later *Rugged* was horizontal. There was no one in sight, and Peter felt easier now because fog had come down mercifully to shroud them. The loom of a light had appeared briefly, and he thought it must have been Cabo Maysi. Perhaps the destroyers were going home and wanted the lighthouse, or, more likely, something was outward bound and coming their way.

He yelled down the voicepipe: "Get a move on and come to full buoyancy! Report when the Air Bottles are full. All departments make your reports."

And so, three hours later, H.M. Nuclear Submarine *Rugged* sank slowly beneath the surface. Shipshape and Bristol fashion, she was once more master of her fate.

"Captain in the Control Room!"

Taggart was at the periscope and he had picked up what he was looking for. Peter took the stick from him.

"Los Frayles, sir, and, slightly to the southward of them, the Alta Vela Islands."

"Yes, I've got 'em, and Beata Island on the far side. That's Cape Beata behind, isn't it?"

"Yes, that's it, sir."

"Well done, Pilot. Come round to the patrol line when Alta Vela is abeam."

"Aye, aye, sir."

The Captain glanced round the Control Room and then returned to the Ward Room for his elevenses. Hank Jefferson was waiting on the settee for him, the poker dice scattered on the table. He was playing 'Beat That!' with Number One and the Chief while they waited for the Captain to join them in a game of 'Liars'. The friendly rattle of the bones was soothing in Peter's ears after the events of the last few hours.

"Aces up, kings towards."

They were off! Hank was renowned for his absurd calling, while the Chief, Engineer Lieutenant Ewan Craig, was of opposite temperament. A man of few words, he was a canny Scot, and he made sure of his call before passing on the dice. He was stocky, with bright blue eyes beneath red eyebrows, and he had a musical lilt to his speech that belonged to Edinburgh.

"Full house, aces on jacks..."

And so the game continued in the Ward Room, the past a nightmare of unreality. In the fore-ends life had returned to normal. Hawkins had his head down and Smith was reading a horror paperback, while at the mess table a game of 'uckers' was in progress. A low laugh escaped for a moment; the comradeship of the confined space was very real during these interludes.

All was quiet in the Petty Officers' Mess. The Coxswain was making up his books but finding difficulty in making his columns tally. He'd lost a tot of rum and couldn't account for it, but the Second Coxswain was taking little interest. He was lost, absorbed in writing a letter to his girl, and even the cockroach that scuttled across the notepaper received a gentle shove. Yes, it was good to be alive and they realised it.

"Captain in the Control Room!"

Peter got up quickly. "What's up, Pilot?" he asked as he reached the nerve centre.

"Asdic operator reports H.E., sir. Says he thinks it's a dived submarine."

"Well, what are you waiting for, Pilot? *Diving stations*!" Peter snapped.

Peter was angry and his face flushed. A few precious seconds had been lost already, and if it wasn't an enemy submarine, what did it matter? He wrenched at the periscope as it flashed past. The dice lay scattered on the Ward Room table as the officers tumbled to their stations: Number One to the planes, the Chief to the Engine Room, Hank to the Tube Space with the Snotty, Geoff Brocklebank to the switchboard and the Sub to his Fruit Machine. The hands scrambled along the passage, groping with their hands and wiping sleep from their eyes.

"Stand by for a fix: Bearing THAT, right-hand edge, Alta Vela; THAT, left-hand edge Beata Island; THAT, Cabo Falso." Peter slammed the handles shut. "Nothing in sight," he said.

Elliott had donned his earphones quickly and he was listening intently as he swivelled the ebonite knob on the dial. Peter was watching him impatiently…

Number One was wrestling with the trim and compensating for the movement of the hands. When the hands were at their diving stations there came a sudden lull.

"All-round sweep completed, sir. Submarine H.E. confirmed, bearing Red one five."

"Surface or dived?"

"Dived. Sorry, sir."

But there was no need for Elliott to apologise. He had worked with Sinclair so long that each man could read the thoughts of the other; they were a natural combination.

"Any idea of range? Up periscope."

"Can't really say unless I transmit, sir."

Peter's heart was pumping against his ribs. This is what he'd been waiting for, and perhaps they were not to be disappointed… The lens pierced the surface, light streamed through a blurred glass, and then the image suddenly cleared. He swept round the horizon: no aircraft. Then he slowly searched each sector, only briefly showing the periscope. The heat shimmered upon an oily sea that stretched away to the lifeless green of the midday coastline. There was nothing in sight.

"Down…"

Something suddenly pierced the glassy surface, about seven hundred yards away. Evil it looked, like a cobra's head…

"Periscope, bearing THAT!"

He slammed the handles shut and the tube slid downwards. There was excitement in his voice.

"Target, U-boat! Transmit, Elliott, and give me a course if you can. Stand by all tubes, Emergency Change of Depth, full ahead!"

The tension mounted in the Control Room. Apart from the relaying of orders, no one spoke while 'Q' was flooded. She cocked up her stern and then she was on her way down.

"All tubes ready, sir!"

"Enemy course about two-six-o, sir, speed eight knots."

"Very good, fire when you come on."

"Aye, aye, sir… Stand by…"

"Fire by time interval," Peter snapped. How easy this was, now that they had homing torpedoes!

"Fire one!" Elliott snapped from his corner.

The boat shook four times, two seconds between each fish. The air rushed back into the boat, hurting the ears, and then the roar of the torpedo's propellers drowned everything. *Rugged* had a good bow-down angle on now and was swinging away fast … seventy, eighty, one hundred feet.

"Two hundred feet, Number One…"

But before Benson could reply, there was a sudden jolt from for'd. They never really knew what happened next, it was so sudden.

Peter was the first to pick himself up from the deck, and his first thought was that they had struck some uncharted rock or had grounded. The boat was rolling drunkenly, and above the crashing of the loose gear there boomed a rasping and tearing noise from for'd. She started to take on a steep bow-down angle. He looked at the gauge and his stomach sank. The pointer was beginning to creep down the dial again. In the recesses of his mind he knew that the decision he would take in the next few seconds would decide their existence…

He'd rammed his enemy, he felt sure of that, for why should *Rugged* go on down if she were aground? With her knife-like bow, *Rugged* must have ripped open her adversary at a broad angle. There was no report of water coming in for'd, so he assumed the U-boat must be impaled on his bows. He wrenched the mike from its socket.

"Any water coming in for'd?" he snapped.

And then, quick as a flash, the loudspeaker crackled with the broad Dorset of the T.I., Petty Officer Slater, the ginger-bearded humorist.

"All tight for'd, sir, but there's something on the end, Lootenant Jefferson thinks."

"Number One, tell the hands to hold their hats on. We're going down."

Then he did a strange thing, one of those instinctive reactions of the born submariner, the only course open to him under the circumstances which could possibly save the boat. He ordered the reverse of the expected.

"Full ahead!"

Number One turned in amazement. What the devil was coming next?

"Hard-a-dive, First Lieutenant. Take her down to one thousand feet."

"One thousand feet, sir. Aye, aye, sir."

The Captain had gone mad. There must be damage for'd and she'd start leaking if she went deep.

"Hard-a-dive, Cox'n. One thousand feet."

The rumble of the propeller now swamped everything except the scrunching of loose metal across the bows.

Rugged must be a good thousand tons heavy by the bow now. The U-boat was stuck on her bows. If Peter couldn't shake her off, both boats would spiral to the bottom locked in mortal embrace... There was little time now, less than thirty seconds perhaps, because the depth was swinging away fast ... six hundred, six-eighty... The pointer was rushing round the dial...

"Shut main ballast Kingstons, shut main vents," Peter ordered. "Blow 'Q'."

The angle was too steep to stand up now, but they were used to this. 'Q' roared as the foul air was vented inboard. Men couldn't hear themselves speak and the stench choked them.

Then nothing but the propeller's pounding was audible as she hurtled downwards... *I suppose he's doing the right thing*, Benson thought numbly, *but God knows what he's up to — it seems suicide to me*. Benson felt sick, and he shut his eyes from the pointers on the gauges. She was falling like a stone. They had never lost depth so quickly and were out of control. The U-boat was taking them with her. The water was deep here and they would fold up like crumpled paper...

Saunders, the Outside E.R.A. stood stolidly by the main vent blows, wheel spanner poised above Number One blow. He guessed the Old Man's action, but he was scared. If the Captain left it too late they'd be crushed to bits, and his eyes turned to the depth gauge: nine hundred feet!

God, I'm frightened, Harry Spink, the eighteen-year-old Sub, whispered to himself. He was pressed against the for'd bulkhead and the knobs of the Fruit Machine were taking lumps out of his back. The boat was almost on its ends now, and above him he saw the Captain folded round the for'd periscope well. Sinclair had turned his face towards the gauge and, as Spink watched, he opened his mouth.

"Stop motor. Full astern!"

The shout carried even above the pandemonium.

Could Thatcher reach the phone…?

"One thousand feet, sir."

By now *Rugged* was nearly vertical. Suddenly Benson understood. The Captain was using the weight of the U-boat to part them. And now that he was taking *Rugged*'s own weight off by going astern on that gigantic propeller, the momentum of the stricken U-boat should separate them. But it had been left too late…

It was very quiet when the motor reduced speed. It stopped, then went astern, and slowly picked up speed. The low-pitched whine grew shriller and then the gearing screamed as the armatures spun at full speed astern.

Eleven hundred feet and still hurtling downwards, on her ends now. Peter Sinclair shut his eyes and his stomach came up to meet him. What a maniac he'd been, what a conceited lunatic — she'd never pull out of this! He longed to blow main ballast but did not dare as yet. Her bows had only to lift slightly and she'd never shake off the crippled enemy…

The for'd phone screamed.

"Water coming in for'd, sir. Through the bow-cap glands," and the Sub's face was white.

The screw was now at full revolutions and the whole boat was shuddering from the torque. Her hull whipped like a trapeze wire, drumming and twanging from the strain. She could not take more…

Her bows sprung suddenly upwards like a catapult. There was a screech of metal for'd, a hideous rending…

"Blow main ballast!"

The scream of high pressure air in the line broke the tension. Each man clung to his self-control, each man had longed to shout the order that could possibly have saved them. Spink had to stuff his knuckles into his mouth to prevent himself yelling, and his hands were bleeding.

"Clear the Tube Space. Shut watertight doors!"

The order cracked like a pistol shot. Men realised suddenly that there was hope and they scrambled to their feet as she levelled off. The bulkhead doors moved and they held on to them like flies to prevent their taking charge as they swung on their hinges. The black clips smacked home and each compartment was on its own.

The fore-end phone buzzed: "Tube Space cleared, sir, watertight door shut."

"Stop blowing."

In the strange silence that followed, only the dreadful breaking-up noises of their adversary could be heard. Men looked into each other's eyes as they listened: it was a mere accident that the tables had not been reversed. They could hear her death throes as she spiralled downwards; the explosions as the trapped air blew away the bulkheads, the shattered airlines screaming, the men trapped in the compartments that still held … the imaginations of those in *Rugged* needed no sharpening. They felt only sorrow for their opposite numbers: hate was one of the emotions that few opposing submariners felt for each other. They knew too well what each had to endure.

Rugged was rocketing to the surface now, her bows tilted upwards steeply … seven hundred feet, six, five, four … one hundred feet.

"Open One main vent."

Peter was smiling. *Rugged* was a live thing with a soul of her own! She was showing them her resilience, her apparent indestructibility, and all aboard shared the same emotion. Out of common hardship the link of trust was forged.

At sixty feet Number One was able to hold her at slow ahead, and after an all-round H.E. sweep Peter took her to periscope depth. The periscope broke surface and the light of day streamed once more into his eyes.

The top of Cabo Beata was just visible, but of the other islands there was no sign.

"I daren't surface yet, Number One. I can see the top of Cape Beata. Starboard fifteen, steer south. Eighty feet, half ahead."

There was a long rumbling beneath them, the reverberations hammering against the pressure hull. In the fore-ends, Hawkins shrugged his shoulders. Another blighter less…

"You're a hard so-and-so, Bill," Ordinary Seaman Smith complained. "You hated the Hun even more."

Hawkins's open face shut like a mask. Anger smouldered in his blue eyes.

"Stow it, Smithy."

Smith resumed his paperback. With the instinct that comes to men who live at close quarters, he realised that he had overstepped the mark.

"Sorry, Bill. I forgot."

The T.I., Petty Officer Rodney Slater, looked on benignly and a slow grin appeared through his straggly red beard. It had been very different a few years back when these two had fought each other under similar circumstances of strain. But it had been foolish of Smith: he should have remembered the facts. Bill Hawkins never forgave the Germans. His wife and kids were dead.

"Wonder when we'll open up to inspect the damage in the Tube Space," said the T.I., and he cocked an eye at the bulkhead door that separated them from the damaged compartment. He'd rimed a small vent near the deckhead and no water had squirted out, so the leak couldn't be too serious. Anyway, if the fore-ends were flooded, the boat would be foundering by now from the added weight at her farthest extremity.

"Stand by to surface. Open all bulkhead doors."

Smith smiled as he replaced the phone. It was good to feel normality returning, although they'd soon settle down again to the round of crises.

Slater looked up at the main vent above their heads. He nodded at Smith.

"Number One main vent checked shut," the seaman, a black-haired youth from Stepney, garbled down the phone.

They felt the bows lifting beneath them, they felt her trembling from the increased speed as she came up from deep, they watched the pointer walk back round the depth gauge, and then they swallowed as the air rushed past them when the upper conning tower hatch was opened. They heard a crashing and then she was wallowing on the surface. Two minutes later the phone buzzed.

"Open Tube Space door and report."

They heard the bilge pumps starting and Slater began knocking the clips off the door. But no water spurted through the joints and, when they opened up, the flood water was barely up to the bottom of the tubes.

The Captain was relieved when he received the report from the Tube Space. He was standing on the fin, Hank Jefferson by his side. Peter was looking impatiently for'd, one eye restlessly searching for aircraft. The Chief was a long time inspecting the damage to the stern. His white figure crouched by the crumpled bows and he seemed to be taking an eternity. Ugly rents were showing and, over the port side, a long sliver of green sheet metal hung drunkenly just for'd of the foreplanes. The Chief returned quickly to the bridge.

"Safe enough to dive, I think, sir," he reported. "But we'll have to return to base. The stern's sprung badly and the foreplanes may jam at any time."

"Thank you, Chief. Tell me more when we dive. I don't like it up here. Hank, get a situation report off to Bermuda, giving them our E.T.A."

The tall American grinned.

"Sorry, sir, but communication's broken down. The aerial's carried away and it'll take a couple of hours to fix."

Peter grinned as he hustled his Liaison Officer down the hatch.

"Dive, dive, dive!" he shouted. "Eighty feet."

CHAPTER 6

The Myrtle Bank

"When can you be ready for sea, Sinclair?"

The Commodore had taken the Captain of the damaged nuclear submarine down to the Cove. There they could talk privately. He wanted to evaluate Sinclair's worth.

"Twenty-four hours after the dockyard have finished, sir. I must do my trial dive first, and, if that's all right, I could be away a day later."

"What day, probably?"

"At a guess, next Tuesday, sir, but you know what the dockyard's like." They both laughed.

"Each day's important now, Sinclair." The Commodore stood on a ledge of coarse grass above the white sand that ran in a crescent round the blue cove. He loved this spot because he could see the shoals of mullet come questing in, the rock cod, and the occasional barracuda. He was a stocky figure, with his hands thrust into the pockets of his white shorts. His epaulets were too heavy for the open-necked white shirt, and they were sloping off his shoulders. But for once he didn't fuss about appearances. He continued talking, his eyes fixed on the water below.

"Our agents report an imminent rebellion, brought on chiefly by the engineered failure of U.N.I.C.E.F. We don't know the date, but we do know that an agent called Brown, a merchant in Kingston, has the key to the information we require. It's vital for me to know when the revolt will take place. I want to know the whereabouts of this Serpent King fellow. I want to know where the Sacred Belt is," and the Commodore watched the young man who stood before him. Sinclair was wiry, thin, and about a foot taller than his senior officer. With light brown hair and grey eyes, there was little outstanding about him unless you took a closer look. Then one could detect the hint of tempered steel that lay beneath the exterior. He was a quiet man and the Commodore noticed that he did not smoke, and when Sinclair gazed at the Commodore, the older man couldn't help feeling that there was something out of the ordinary here. A sound man, he judged, and then the chap would smile and the illusion would change. His face would light up in mischievous fun, as his eyes wrinkled at the corners with tiny crow's feet. He had a reputation for being a menace at a party, but it was only when he smiled that you saw this side of him. *A man of many parts*, thought the Commodore.

"What do you want *Rugged* to do, sir?"

There was no insolence in the query. Just a plain question.

"Wait for it, my boy! I haven't quite finished yet." The older man smiled before continuing:

"There's been a new development. The swine have captured the Bishop of the Antilles. At least, that's the best information we have. He's a fine, middle-aged man, particularly loved by his people because he's one of them himself. He's a militant, outspoken man and he has been hitting back at the insidious tactics of the infiltrators. He was beginning to rally the natives when the Commies got him: he was too dangerous."

The Commodore kicked viciously at a lump of coral and it went spinning over the edge of the cliff. The pool rippled below them.

"We haven't heard of him for over a month. We reckon the enemy are brainwashing him and trying to get him to confess to complicity in the food scandals and in spying... But it just shows the hold the Commies have got over the population: the natives have deserted even their well-loved Lord Bishop for the nightmare world of this Serpent King and his fiendish Sacred Belt."

"What are we doing about it, sir? Wait to see what's going to happen, as usual?"

The Commodore looked up sharply. "For once we're going to take action, Sinclair. At least you are."

Peter gazed out to sea. He would always remember this moment. This was the moment he'd been waiting for, the reason he'd been summoned to Admiralty House.

"The enemy have always been one jump ahead," the Commodore continued. "Their intelligence seems much better than ours, and so we've always started at a disadvantage… They seem to know our every move, and that doesn't help. But now we've decided to beat them at their own game." He paused as he looked at Peter. "Listen carefully, for these orders are not even committed to paper. Of course, you can turn them down if you think they're a bit beyond you." He smiled as he watched the young man's reaction.

"As I mentioned earlier, we have an agent named Brown, and he is waiting for one of us to contact him at the Myrtle Bank Hotel in Kingston. He refuses to part with the information that will lead us to the Serpent King and his Sacred Belt. I think the reason is obvious and that Brown is wise: too much has been compromised already."

"What is this Belt, sir?"

"Don't really know for sure. It's some sort of fetish which the Serpent King uses as a symbol. He has built around it all the hideous paraphernalia of savagery upon which this movement thrives. It doesn't seem possible, does it, my boy, for these carefree and happy people to lose their heads like this?"

"It's happened before, sir. Remember how the Congo started and how out of that chaos U.N.O. was really born? Lies and falsehood are eventually seen through."

"One of you must contact Brown. His office is Taylor and Brown's, near the Myrtle Bank Hotel. This is the identification procedure: Brown parts his hair on the right. You are to do the same. After you've asked him if he's Mr. Brown, you will offer him a cigar. He will take it, remove the band and remark, 'I don't usually smoke in Lent.' Then he will look at the band and add: 'But I smoke only Havanas.' You are to reply, 'Jamaicans are just as good.'

"That is the drill and you must memorise it perfectly, because he won't disclose himself unless the procedure is correct."

"'Jamaicans are just as good,'" Peter repeated. "I'll remember that."

"Good. Here are your orders: First. You yourself are not to land at Kingston. You are to remain in command of *Rugged* off Kingston. You must send someone else for this part of the exercise. Jefferson, your Liaison Officer perhaps. He's done this sort of thing before, I believe."

"Yes, he has, sir. But he's American. Does that matter?"

"Why the devil should it?" the Commodore snapped.

"With his Yankee accent he might be more open to suspicion. And besides, Jamaica's still nominally a British possession."

The elder man laughed. Sinclair was still thinking in the past.

"You're more of a square than I am! At least I'm reconciled to the idea that this is a U.N.O. show, not a British one. You'd better revise your ideas, Sinclair. The days of Empire are over and the planet belongs to us all now — by kind permission of the totalitarians."

"Right, sir. I'll send Lieutenant Jefferson."

The Commodore continued: "When you recover the American, he will have the information to enable you to contact the Serpent King. Spy mania is rampant in the West Indies, so you'll need your wits about you.

"Second. You are to capture the Serpent King and the Sacred Belt. Both are to be brought back to Bermuda, the King preferably alive.

"Third. You are to discover the root cause of the failure of U.N.I.C.E.F. Ten thousand pounds in cash is waiting for you in the Supply Officer's office. You'll need it for emergencies; pick it up when you go."

The Commodore had turned his back on the sea and was beginning to climb the steep slope to Admiralty House.

"This operation is vital to the West Indies, Sinclair. If you're successful we may still save them. These people are now living in a hideous nightmare and somehow they've got to be brought back to sanity. If they're not, we lose the West Indies, the Caribbean and possibly the whole free world. Our enemies are throwing in everything they have, so you can see the importance they attach to this particular front. The chances are slim, and I must emphasise that if you're captured, H.M. Government can do nothing to save you — they may even spurn you and refuse to recognise you. But if you win, Sinclair," and the older man turned round and placed his hand firmly on Peter's shoulder. "If you win, the happiness of millions of humble souls will be your reward."

The Commodore coughed. He turned abruptly and continued up the shaded grass between the cedars.

"This isn't a direct order, Sinclair. You may refuse if you wish and no one will think any the worse of you. You have until noon tomorrow to make up your mind."

"Thank you, sir, but I'd like to go."

Then the Commodore's steps scrunched on the gravel which surrounded the house.

"Collect the cash, Sinclair. Good luck," he grunted. But he did not look back.

The glare from the white walls of the dockyard hurt Peter's eyes as he gazed up at the shining hull... He stood on the deck of the floating dock, looking up at *Rugged*. Perched in the air, she seemed an unwieldy lump of metal, but even now you could tell she was no ordinary boat. Large, temporary pipes led over the bulging hull and from her port side a continuous sea discharge cascaded. Her huge central propeller gleamed in the sunlight and the anti-fouling shone as it started to dry. The dock was flooding down in half an hour and already the dockyard mateys were beginning to assemble in laughing groups.

He strolled for'd to inspect the bows. No damage was to be seen now, and Peter marvelled at their luck. He may have sunk an enemy submarine, but so easily it could have been the other way about. He climbed up the steel ladders of the deck in thoughtful mood and crossed the brow that stretched to his ship. The jib of a crane swung above him, waiting to remove the gangway, while fifty feet below him he saw the water starting to engulf the floor of the dock. With a sigh of relief he climbed the fin to watch developments. He hardly noticed Number One waiting for him.

"All hands on board, sir. Ready for sea."

The Chief saluted.

"All openings checked shut, sir. Repairs completed satisfactorily."

The Captain returned the salute but he said little until *Rugged* had left the dockyard. The submarine had stored, refuelled and reloaded with torpedoes. She was now turning for The Narrows and for the Atlantic where she was to carry out her deep dive to test the repairs to her bows. The wake boiled suddenly at her stern and she slid between the arms of the yellow breakwaters. The blue-green waterway to Hamilton opened up before her, and Ireland Island began to fade astern. She left Hogfish Beacon abeam to starboard and then picked up the black cone of Number 29 buoy. The seamen were fallen in on the fore-casing, and as the submarine slid past the white flagstaff at Clarence Cove, he saw a stocky figure waving with his cap. The shrill piping of a bosun's call drifted across the water and the hands sprung to attention. Peter saluted a moment, and with a wide flourish of his arm returned the Commodore's farewell.

"Fall out harbour stations, Number One. Secure for sea."

The green and mauve of the north shore slid quickly past and hardly had the First Lieutenant gone below than they reached The Narrows. Peter glimpsed 'Arcadia's' roof behind a clump of cedars and he felt sad at leaving the battered Mess. He wondered if he'd see it again … and then he turned to the job in hand.

"Stand by for the Trim Dive."

He took a last look at St. Georges but could not sight Tom Hillyard's schooner. He was on a surveying trip and Peter was sorry to have missed him.

And so, less than an hour later, *Rugged* was at periscope depth and taking her departure for the Windward Passage. The deep dive was successful and there was no leak from for'd. Peter summoned his officers into the Ward Room and briefed them.

"We are bound for Kingston, Jamaica," he was saying. "And I hope to be off Port Royal around sunset the day after tomorrow," he went on. "So you, Hank, have got plenty of time to prepare yourself for the shock!"

Then Peter elaborated his plans in detail. A folboat had been smuggled aboard during the night in the dockyard, and two packing cases had arrived for the 'Commanding Officer (Personal)'.

"In those crates, Hank, is a complete wardrobe for you and the man who is to escort you in the folboat. You've got to disguise yourself as a broken-down sugar planter."

"Shouldn't be difficult," murmured Number One.

"Would you like to take Hawkins with you?" Peter asked, grinning broadly. "He may come in handy."

The Windward Passage was safely negotiated at five hundred feet, and *Rugged* made her landfall off Port Royal at sunset two days later. She had deliberately avoided the congested enemy shipping that was steaming in a continuous stream from Kingston and Cuba to the West Indies.

Peter was at the periscope as the sun disappeared behind the jagged line of the Blue Mountains that were mauve and transparent with distance. The crimson ball sent diverging shafts of golden colour streaming across the sky and Peter let the Control Room crew watch the marvel through the periscope. It had been sticky all day and now that the sun had gone, it might perhaps become cooler.

"Stand by for a fix. Then I'll bottom her until 0200, and we can all get our heads down. Down periscope."

"All right for some," croaked an American voice by the W/T office. "But I'm not figuring on hitting the hay. I sorta got something on my mind."

Peter looked at the tall man in the corner. He was dressed in crumpled whites, he had not shaved for two days, and there were grey shadows beneath his eyes. His suit hung loosely from him in rumpled, grubby folds. A yellow handkerchief protruded defiantly from the breast pocket. He was down on his luck, and it looked as if the bottle already had him in its clutches.

"Is Hawkins ready with the folboat?"

"Yes, sir," the 'planter' replied. "It's out of the torpedo rack and standing by in the fore-ends. Hawkins is looking forward to it, I reckon."

"Up periscope. You'd better have a last look before the light goes, Hank. D'you see where that narrow strip of land, which is protecting the main harbour, joins the mainland? You'll land there. That scrub will give you good cover, and Hawkins can lie up there for you all day. You can rejoin him tomorrow night and I'll be waiting for you here. The moon doesn't rise before 2330, so you will have an hour and a half in darkness in which to find us. I'll be flashing with the infrared Aldis. Here, come and have a look."

The periscope slipped upwards a further nine inches for the lanky American and he took a long look along the bearing of his intended landing place. He grunted and the periscope slid downwards when he'd finished identifying the spot. He knew it by heart now; he'd been looking at it since they closed the harbour. He saw the yellow and white of the wharves along the waterfront, and above them, in the foothills, the residences of the well-to-do. He could pick out the barracks of the local militia, cool beneath the palms, but no Union Jack flew from the flagstaff now. The troops had defected two years ago, the officers had been shot, and now the Peoples' Militia used the buildings as a training centre. The long spur that curved outside the harbour was covered with green scrub, and *Rugged* could bottom close in here without fear of detection. Admittedly she would have little water above her, but as no ship came down this end of the spur, she was safe. They could pick out the outline of the broken-down masonry of the old harbour of Port Royal, once the dockyard that had careened Nelson's ships when he was searching for Villeneuve's French fleet. Today's channel led round the western end of this spur and threaded its way through the treacherous shallows which lay between Port Royal and the Kingston jetties. At the eastward end of the town the Myrtle Bank Hotel was visible, it's roof peeping between the palms that waved in the evening breeze. There Hank would contact Mr. Brown.

"Good luck, Hank."

"Thank you, sir. See you tomorrow night."

The American vaulted lightly over the fin and clambered down to the folboat bobbing alongside, Able Seaman Hawkins being in the forward berth. He was fending the canvas canoe off from the rounded hull, while the Second Coxswain tended the heaving line. Number One was there to see them off.

"So long, chum."

It was very dark. From the fin Peter could barely see the First Lieutenant's arm signalling that the folboat was clear.

"Slow astern."

Hank and Bill Hawkins rested on their paddles while they watched the black juggernaut sliding astern into the night. In a few seconds she had disappeared and then they heard her main vents blowing. There was silence and suddenly they felt very much alone.

"Come on, Bill. Let's get going."

The paddles moved as one. The folboat swayed as she gathered way and then all that could be heard was the dripping of the blades as they left the water. Hank guided her towards the dark line of low-lying scrub, and then suddenly they saw a white line of surf breaking gently along the shore. Hank lifted his paddle from the water. Bill stopped paddling and they both listened while the folboat drifted inshore. Hank cocked his head and then he heard the pounding of the waves upon the sand. He started paddling again and took her in to fifty yards. He turned her to the eastward and they took her parallel to the low-lying spit. The canoe was invisible in the darkness, and even if sentries had been posted on this outlandish peninsula, they would have found difficulty in finding the intruder. A flight of wildfowl burst from the mud right ahead of him, mewing and screaming in the blackness, and Hank's heart missed a beat. But at last they reached a point where the arm joined the mainland and they slowed their paddling.

Hank spotted a break in the foreshore and they ran her towards it. Bill Hawkins felt the soft mud under his paddle and he vaulted silently from the bows. He waded inshore and hauled on the painter until she'd come no more. He felt hard bottom under his feet, and when she would not budge he went aft to help Hank. The 'planter' could not enter Kingston covered in mud.

"Right, sir."

And so, in the early hours of Tuesday, a dissolute planter might have been seen, carried piggyback by a British sailor, landing in the swamps to the south of Kingston. But no man would have cared to reconnoitre this lonely reach and no one saw them.

"Good luck, sir. I'll be waiting for you here from dark onwards."

"Thanks, Bill. So long." The grey figure slunk into the darkness. Hawkins returned slowly to the folboat and hauled her into the coarse grass which grew above high-water mark. She slid easily until he reached the scrub and then he hid himself in the swamp.

Hank moved towards the higher ground. The top of a sea wall showed in front of him and he scrambled up its bank. From the top he could just see the sweep of water curving away into the harbour, the long spit of scrub forming a protective arm from the surge of the Caribbean. It was comforting to know that Bill was waiting for him, hidden in the swamp. Already the streaks of first light were beginning to slash the eastern sky with the cold greens and silvers of another dawn. It was barely three-thirty, yet light was filtering through the cumulus, silver-shot in the sky. Then Hank realised he'd been fooled. Stealing from behind a bank of cloud was the moon, not yet past its quarter.

The Blue Mountains seemed absurdly close as he lengthened his stride towards them. He walked fast, intending to reach the outskirts of Kingston before daylight. But when he neared the mainland, he realised that he would have to lie up for awhile: he did not relish stumbling into a patrol in the darkness. As soon as he was sure of his way, he looked for somewhere to lay his head for a couple of hours. If he was discovered, he would be living the part even better: a besotted down-and-out, sleeping off a heavy night. A collection of hovels lay not far to his right, and from one of them a trail of blue smoke was already curling upwards. The natives had to be up early and he could see a dog prowling round a heap of garbage. Then the wretched creature pricked up its ears and sniffed in Hank's direction. Hank sank slowly to the ground and held his breath. He must be upwind of the pie-dog and Hank cursed beneath his breath. How careless he'd been!

Then he heard a yelping and a scuffling through the goosegrass. He heard the animal panting and then two red eyes were glinting at him, the animal's ruff standing stiffly. Hank thought quickly. He was discovered, and if he antagonised the brute, the whole neighbourhood would know of it. He snapped his fingers and softly beckoned the dog. He felt in his pocket and snatched out a Horlicks tablet, part of his action ration pack. The cur slunk towards him, smelt him, and then nuzzled its head against his thigh. Hank patted the bony animal and together they approached the hovels. An interested old man stood watching them. He was scratching about in the dirt, laying the morning fire. The smell brought home to Hank the nostalgic memories of the pinewoods way back home.

"Good morning, Johnny," Hank said grumpily. "Dunno how I got out here! Can you put me on the right road to town?"

The old man looked at him in disgust. He did not smile as he looked the white man up and down. He jerked his thumb over his shoulder and spat. *Strange*, thought Hank, *but there's hate in the old fellow's eyes...* The Jamaican clucked his tongue and the cur crept between his legs. They both watched the American as he disappeared down the dirt track that led towards the main road. Hank did not look back. He could feel more than one pair of eyes watching him as he ambled nonchalantly away from the hovels.

The sun climbed rapidly from behind the seaward horizon and Hank felt his spirits lift with the promise of the day's work. He'd been depressed by the black man's reaction, but the old jerk could hardly be blamed for assuming the worst. Hank smiled as he glanced down at his stained whites; he stroked his face and felt the stubble on his cheeks. He must be looking disreputable! What wouldn't he give for a shave and a decent breakfast just at this minute! He fished a slab of chocolate from his pocket.

It was ten o'clock when he decided to enter Kingston. The sun was well into the sky with its promise of midday heat. It was sticky and muggy, and mirages shimmered above the dusty road. Hank's feet were tired, so there was now no need to feign weariness. He dragged his steps as he entered the main street of Kingston, and he didn't recoil when the cars rattled by, clouds of dust whirling behind them.

He noticed the ramshackle hovels that lay behind the facade of the shopping centre. Boys chased each other amongst the fowls, and grey washing hung between the corrugated iron roofs of the shanties. He turned up a side street and went into a sub-post office. A kindly face peered at him from behind a grille, but Hank saw the momentary shadow of fear that crossed the old woman's glistening countenance.

"Can I help you, sah?"

Hank looked around the shop and asked for razor blades, while the postmistress looked on disapprovingly.

"How much?"

He paid for the blades and, as he turned to go, he asked if she could direct him to Taylor and Brown's, the merchants.

"Taylor and Brown's? Yassir. Opposite de Myrtle Bank — anyone show you."

Hank stumbled into the glare of the sun again when he reached the main street. The heat hit him and he lashed out at the flies swarming round his sweating forehead. There was something strange about the town, a feeling of fear, of hate, of a furtive secretiveness. How different it had all been a few years ago, when he'd flown down from Newport News for a weekend on a U.N.O. fact-finding commission! The inhabitants had been a happy, smiling bunch, eager to help…

He felt himself pushed suddenly into the gutter. He stumbled, then saw two youths. They were strongly built thugs in their early twenties. They laughed as they watched him, and yelled as they swaggered on their way, "White trash!"

Hank swallowed. He resisted the impulse to give chase but instead he played the part of shamed bravado. He dusted himself down and continued up the road, keeping to the gutter. The pavement walkers taunted him, but the older folk looked away. Then he saw the Myrtle Bank Hotel, still white and impressively remote from the sordid world it shared with other mortals.

A commissionaire still stood outside, white and splendid in the shade of the portals, but above him the facade was covered with enormous photographs of a grim and humourless personage. He was staring at you as you walked down the street. 'Down with the Fascist Colonisers! We want Freedom! Long Live the Serpent King! Death to Traitors!' the placards exhorted.

But there were few people, Hank noticed, who paid attention to the announcements. No one looked up; they were intent on their business and seemed in a hurry to pass this area as quickly as possible. Several policemen were grouped in the shade of the white columns in front of the hotel. Many of the men walking down the street were wearing red armbands. There was an arrogant air about them and they were probably the local militia. Hank shivered as he felt the miasma of mistrust about him: the Commies had certainly taken over here! The populace were forced to enjoy the usual trappings of this soulless regime. He was relieved when he saw the nameboard of Taylor and Brown staring at him from the sidewalk opposite the Myrtle Bank. The sunblinds were drawn. He went into the entrance hall of the merchants' premises and blinked in the sudden gloom.

"Can I help you, sah?"

The tone was bantering, sarcastic, and the face was sneering. The porter who was barring the way to the enquiries desk had already decided to evict this unsavoury planter: the white trash had probably come to ask for more credit and couldn't even pay his account.

"I'd like to see Mr. Brown — Mr. Christopher Brown."

"What name, sah? Is he expecting you, sah?" The porter looked Hank up and down insolently. "I don't think he's in, sah."

"He's expecting me," Hank whined, fighting back his anger. "Tell him it's Tony Waddell and I have some cigars for him."

The porter hesitated and then he noticed anger stirring in the planter's eyes. Perhaps the Old Man was expecting him? He sniffed, turned on his heel and went to the desk where he picked up a telephone. He leant on the mahogany top and stared at Hank as he contacted the secretary. Hank watched the man's face scowling, but when the porter returned there was a trace of servility.

"Mr. Brown will see you now, sah. Dis way, please."

Brown's office was above and Hank climbed the gloomy stairs. The porter knocked deferentially, his ear strained to the heavy mahogany panel. Then he flung open the door with a flourish.

"*Mister* Waddell, sah." He gave Hank a look of hate as he ushered him into the inner sanctum. Hank swallowed as he entered the office. This was the moment when anything might happen and his mind raced for the password.

"Good morning, Mr. Waddell, I've been expecting you," a silky voice greeted from the corner by the green sunblind.

A heavy, middle-aged man was watching Hank's entry. His hair was parted on the right side of his head and Hank saw his eyes flicker as they recognised the similar affectation of his own. The merchant stood poised upon the balls of his feet and kept one hand firmly in the pocket of his ample drill jacket. Hank smoothed down his hair with the palm of his hand.

"Mr. Brown?" the American asked.

The man nodded but stayed his distance.

"Cigar?" Hank asked, as he held out his case.

The revolving fan above their heads whirled steadily. Hank carefully watched his man. Mr. Brown stretched out his hand, then he sniffed the cigar, twirling it between his fingers.

"I don't usually smoke in Lent," he said.

Mr. Brown was looking at Hank from beneath his eyebrows. He snapped off the band and it fell to the floor. "But I smoke only Havanas," he added.

Hank was grinning now. This was idiotic!

"Jamaicans are just as good," he replied, the tension slipping from him.

Brown moved to the door and turned the key. He beckoned Hank to a chair.

"Sinclair?"

"No. My name's Jefferson, sir. Peter Sinclair sent me on his behalf."

The merchant was an ageing man. Heavily built, he slumped behind his desk with a sigh. He looked across at the American with frightened eyes.

"I've got to kick you out in twenty minutes' time. I've an appointment with the Police Inspector and he mustn't sight you. Let me do the talking, eh?" The white-haired merchant smiled quickly. Hank relaxed in the chair.

"The uprising in the whole of the Federation is imminent, Jefferson. Although the insurrection is largely controlled from here, the emphasis is shifting to the Islands. The Commies are organised and are pouring the stuff in: arms, agents and troops. I couldn't risk getting in touch with your people, so that's why I asked you to contact us."

He rose from his desk and moved to the window. He pulled the cord of the sunblind and the slats shut out the light. He snapped on a wall light and the effect was depressing in this sweltering heat.

"Just while we talk," he apologised. "The Turtle Tank's too close and we may be overlooked."

Hank wished he'd get on with it for he was trickling with perspiration. He felt trapped.

"A Colonel Platt is organising all resistance in the Virgin Islands. Ten days ago I heard from him that he has discovered the date and place for the outbreak of the revolt. A wireless transmission is too easily monitored in these small islands, so I sent an agent to him. But poor Henri never got there." He sighed. "His throat was cut."

"Where does Colonel Platt live, sir?"

"On the island of Tortola. His house lies above the bay and is the only decent habitation. He grows molasses. You are to contact him and then you must act. I wish to goodness I knew..." The harassed man ran his fingers through his hair and looked straight through Hank. He spoke like a drugged man, fighting feebly against something larger than life, something that overwhelmed him, something evil, monstrous.

"You'll find things a nightmare, horrible and unreal, Jefferson. These happy people have been seduced by this cult of the Serpent King's. When they see the Sacred Belt they are back in their primeval forests, lusting for blood." He glanced at the American who sat quietly in front of him.

"This Belt is the symbol of freedom. When exhibited it is the sign for human sacrifice. The Serpent King is in the Islands now, whipping up last-minute fervour for the day of the uprising."

"And Colonel Platt knows the date of the uprising and where the Serpent King can be found?"

"That's right, my friend. You've only to contact him."

"Same password?"

"Yes. But I'm afraid I must hurry you now. You mustn't bump into our Chief Butcher. Better leave by the rear entrance."

Mr. Brown rose ponderously from his desk and opened a door at the side of the room.

"Good luck, Jefferson, and God bless you. Your organisation is our last hope."

Hank shook hands.

"One thing, sir. Is Colonel Platt expecting us?"

"Yes, my boy. He's expecting you," the frightened merchant murmured. "He's expecting you."

CHAPTER 7

Tortola

Peter Sinclair was glad to be clear of Jamaica. Lying bottomed all day in those shallows had been infernally sticky and uncomfortable. He'd been relieved to recover Hank and Bill Hawkins without a hitch. The infrared drill had worked perfectly and they'd even picked up the folboat without damage. Peter breathed more freely when the hatch was shut fast again and they were beneath the surface. *Rugged* went to eighty feet as soon as there was enough water under her, and then she set course for Tortola.

Hank and Peter Sinclair had met for a brief talk as soon as they were clear, when the American gave them their destination.

"Tortola?" Peter asked, trying to recall the place. "Surely that's the island the buccaneers used, isn't it? It's right at the top of the West Indies, one of the Virgin Islands." He moved across to the chart. "I was there as a midshipman and nearly broke my leg falling down a hole. The island is stiff with ancient caches which the pirates are supposed to have used to bury their treasure."

"A Colonel Platt is our man, sir. We're to contact him and he will give us the information. Apparently things are pretty tense in the islands. From what I gathered they were bad enough in Kingston."

"You'd better get your head down, Hank. We'll lay our plans when you wake up. I'll press on for Tortola."

Ian Taggart was laying off a course for Mona Island, the islet which guards the Mona Passage. The First Lieutenant was on watch.

"Better come and share this, Number One. I'm leaving you in command while I go ashore here."

Peter had thought long about this possibility. Benson was competent. If he was forbidden to fire at targets, he could carry out a reconnaissance adequately.

"I shall go north-about for Tortola. At this speed, provided we don't run into trouble, we should make the Mona Passage during daylight tomorrow afternoon. But we shall have to be careful: two destroyer squadrons are operating from Santo Domingo and San Juan. Tell the Officer of the Watches to keep a good look out. I don't want a repetition of the Windward Passage lark!"

The Captain exchanged the chart for the Virgin Islands group, and the crisp paper looked at first glance to be peppered with markings. Christopher Columbus discovered this group of over one hundred islands on his second voyage in 1494. Life on them had changed little.

"Here is Tortola, and we shall run into Road Harbour, taking transits here, Pilot. We'll land in our folboat here, on this beach, to the left of the village, and you'll surface here, Number One, to dispatch us."

Benson looked carefully, and then the Captain exchanged the chart for the small-scale one of the Eastern Caribbean. His finger ran down to the southern edge where he found Trinidad.

"Patrol here, Number One, off the Boca Grande until you hear from me. Record all shipping movement but do *not* disclose your position or fire torpedoes."

Benson looked dejected, but he understood. He must not jeopardise the submarine or the chance of retrieving the Captain and his party. After all, he'd not had the experience of a wartime attack yet.

"Who's going with you, sir?" asked Taggart hopefully.

"Hank and Hawkins. I've got to leave the boat in capable hands, Pilot." Peter smiled. Taggart hated to miss the fun.

By late afternoon they had picked up Cape Beata, the promontory which had so nearly marked their grave. When the Cape was abeam, *Rugged* reduced speed in order to make a landfall on Mona Island at daybreak. She went deep during the night when all hands snatched some sleep. Two ships came near at 2.20 a.m., on a westerly course. They sounded uncommonly like destroyers as they rumbled overhead, but *Rugged* continued undetected. It was a nasty moment, however, and Peter was glad to be woken at last by the midshipman, Michael O'Donovan. Not yet eighteen, he was shaping up well. Peter took in the pale face that was peering down at him. The light had snapped on in his tiny sea-cabin, and with the pressure of the Snotty's hand on his shoulder, Peter had jerked awake immediately. Dark eyes glittered above him, and Peter noticed the weariness that showed around the young man's eyes. O'Donovan had been at school less than a year ago but was finding this man's world much to his liking.

"Officer of the Watch's compliments, sir. Dawn is breaking and Saona Island is in sight. Request permission to alter to o-seven-o when it's abeam?"

Peter grunted and O'Donovan left the cabin quietly, carefully drawing the Admiralty pattern curtain after him. The maroon cloth hung from brass rings, and all his life Peter would associate the noise of their scraping along the bar with these nightly intrusions. He dragged himself from his bunk, stretched, yawned and combed his hair. This was likely to be a hectic day and he wondered what it would bring. This routine was tuning him again to the pitch he'd known once before; to the pitch when one's instincts warned of danger even before it happened. He clambered down to the Control Room.

"Good morning, sir." Brocklebank was smiling smugly. He'd picked up his landfall right ahead.

Peter snapped his fingers. The periscope slid upwards and he made a quick all-round look. No aircraft, no ships in sight. He sighed with relief as he changed to low power. He didn't want to be hunted in this relatively narrow passage that lay ahead of them. Mona Island should be due east of them now, and he took a long look at the land that lay to the northward.

The republic of Dominica lay at the eastern end of the island that neighboured Cuba, the first Communist conquest. It seemed a long time ago now since that puppet took the island over from the dictator Batista. What was his name...? Castro, that was it, but that had been way back in the late fifties. Peter smiled grimly as he peered at the dark shores of the island that was once named Hispaniola and which had been christened by Columbus in 1492, in honour of his powerful neighbour at home. So *New Spain* it became. To the westward lay the other half of the island, its mauve mountains towering in the distance. This was Haiti, the Country of the Mountains. But the natives of Haiti still viewed their neighbours in Dominica with distrust, and well they might, after the massacres instituted by that savage dictator of earlier days, Trujillo. Santo Domingo had long been a prize worthy of attention for those with designs on America. Long before the Communists, came the Nazis in the 1930s; they also laid greedy eyes on the island as a springboard. But now the Red Flag flew throughout the island.

"Down periscope."

At eleven, Mona Island was in sight and by noon it was abeam to starboard and less than three miles away. Now enemy-held, it shot perpendicularly from the deeps, its flat top fringed with green scrub. It looked toy-like from a distance, but the gun emplacements and the lighthouse soon dispelled the illusion.

"Silent Routine, Number One. They may have hydrophones out here."

And so by late afternoon, *Rugged* was safely through the passage. Four more destroyers passed to the north-westward in the evening, and Peter watched them disappearing in a flurry of white spume. He returned to his game of uckers.

"Well, Hank, are we all ready for the landing tonight?"

The American had altered since his first Commando days in Malta. No longer puffy under the eyes, he was a seasoned campaigner, tough, wiry and alert. He had retained his sense of humour, but he was more reserved now. His long fingers gripped the leather pot and he shook the dice.

"Two sixes — ha!"

He moved the yellow counter on top of another and put down the pot.

"Yes, sir, we're all set. Bill Hawkins says we're to look after you!" and his eyes twinkled as he looked at his Captain. There was a strong bond between these two men, fused in the heat of action. Hank Jefferson had been tempered by the British submariners and he now understood them better.

Peter rolled … a double one! There was a hoot of derision.

"I'm reckoning to land at about 0200, Hank. Can the three of us fit in the folboat?"

"Sure, sir. It can be adapted for three by shifting the seating batons. I've already fixed that."

"We can't take too much gear. A gun each and the money will be about all we can manage."

"I've seen the belts the Cox'n has made, sir," Taggart chipped in. "We ought to be able to take all the money in those."

"Yes, we'll divide the notes between us in case we're separated," Peter said. He chuckled when he saw that everyone was smiling. "You'll probably never see us again!" he added.

Only the rattle of the dice could be heard in the silence that followed.

"Form a barrier, sir," Taggart said quietly to his Captain, and he moved one of the red counters. "You nearly missed that one."

And so the long day dragged by; the nearer zero hour approached, so the tension heightened. Little was said in the Ward Room after they surfaced at sunset. The Captain was on the bridge, conning the boat close along the northern shores of the islands of St. Thomas and St. John. The ex-Danish island of Charlotte Amalie was astern now, and Tortola was emerging from the darkness ahead. The outline of the island rose higher from the sea than its neighbours, and already Peter could pick out Road Harbour through his night glasses.

"I shall have to go in on the surface. Take over when we reach the dropping position, Number One."

"Aye, aye, sir. After I leave you, I'll keep east of the Leeward Islands on my way down to the Boca Grande."

The Captain was crouching over the compass and fixing the ship. "Good luck, Number One. Hope to rejoin you soon, but this trip may take longer than expected. If we haven't contacted you within the month, you are to return to Bermuda as ordered. Under no circumstances are you to hazard the ship on our behalf, do you understand?"

Benson said nothing. For so long Sinclair and he had worked together. He couldn't realise that this might well be their last conversation. He'd been a good Captain, and Benson forgave him his weakness of temper. He hit with his torpedoes and that's what mattered to a submariner.

"I understand, sir."

Sinclair straightened himself from the compass and passed the bearings down the voicepipe. He adjusted the course and watched the island drawing nearer. *Rugged* was trimmed well down, only the fin being visible. This black smudge, sliding through the darkness, was difficult to sight.

The land seemed very close now. There was no light on the island: the enemy were taking hostilities seriously. The hills looked down menacingly upon the intruder. The sea was calm and its oily blackness undulated across the bay.

"Stop motor," Peter said quietly, "slow astern."

The beach party were already on the fore-casing. Peter could feel the blows of the sledgehammer as the fore-ends crew tried to take off the clips of the fore-hatch. A circular red glow appeared in the fore-casing and then Peter heard the whispering of Jack Weston, the Second Coxswain, as he struggled with the folboat. In less than a minute it was through the hatch and slithering into the water on the ends of heaving lines. The red aperture disappeared and the boat shuddered again as the clips were smacked home.

Benson shook hands, and without another word the Captain climbed down the fin. Benson saluted in the darkness as he watched his commanding officer clamber into the bobbing folboat. He could see the dark figures of Hank and Hawkins reaching out to help their Captain. The heaving lines flopped back on the deck and then the folboat disappeared towards the shore. Benson was on his own.

"Red one hundred, sir. Dark object!"

Benson spun round towards the signalman. He stood above the man and lined up his binoculars immediately over Goddard's. He swung his glasses slowly across the horizon line, but there was nothing. It was so dark that it was difficult to distinguish between sky and water, but he cut back again up the port side. There was something there, darker than the remainder of his field of vision; just a smudge, a suspicion. He pressed his eyes into the rubber eyepiece, blinked to clear his eyes and cut back again. Ah! Goddard was right, there *was* something and his heart leapt. At least two darkened ships were creeping towards *Rugged* and from this angle they could be destroyers in line ahead.

"Half ahead, hard-a-starboard!" the new Captain shouted down the voicepipe. "Dive, dive, dive!"

The three men in the folboat suddenly felt very much alone. They could pick out the entrance to the bay, but little else. And then Peter, who was sitting between the two paddlers, heard Benson's voice, shouting in the night. There was the noise of a swirling propeller and the typical rumbling sound of *Rugged* turning in a tight circle.

What the devil is she up to? thought Peter. *Surely there's no need for that?* Then he tried to stop criticising his First Lieutenant. After all, Peter hadn't given him much chance of handling ship yet, had he?

The swish of the paddles in the darkness was the only sound now, and it was so dark that Peter could barely see the outline of the shore. Bill's back blocked the view ahead and all Peter could do was to search for the westward arm of the bay that was called Road Harbour. The folboat was moving fast now;

she rolled from the thrust imparted by the paddlers, but not a drop of water was shipped.

In the bows, Bill stopped paddling suddenly. He pointed with his left arm over the port bow, and while Peter peered anxiously in that direction, Hank searched all round. Bill had sighted something ahead, but Peter couldn't pick it out yet. Peter felt a tap on his shoulder and turned round.

"For God's sake, sir, look!" the American whispered hoarsely.

A destroyer's silhouette was sliding silently across the mouth of the bay. She was so close that she filled the horizon. They were downwind of her and Peter could smell the stench of fuel-oil and could hear her boiler room fans whining.

They started paddling furiously towards the low-lying spur of beach. The paddles thrashed madly and the folboat nearly capsized from the sudden rolling. Bill held water. The canoe spun round and headed for a white ribbon of sand which seemed very close. A few strokes and Bill felt the bottom under his paddle. He held up his arms and Hank allowed the canoe to drift inshore. Bill clambered out and hauled the folboat ashore by the painter. Hank ripped its canvas with his Commando knife and they steadied it for a moment until it was awash. Then they shoved it out into the sea.

There was a vivid flash in the sky over the bay and, as they looked upwards, a shower of sparks tumbled below the cloud; the star shell fell slowly, pirouetting downwards and throwing weird shadows against the low nimbus. Another, then another star shell burst, until the whole bay was as light as day. The destroyers were using flashless cordite: only the crash of the guns betrayed their whereabouts.

"Just in time," Peter whispered. "*Rugged* must have dived. There can't be much water under her. But if Number One gives her full speed she may get away with it. The destroyers are at a disadvantage in the bay."

"They'll get in each other's way, won't they, sir?" Bill Hawkins muttered from the rough coral rock. The three men had flattened themselves when the first shell exploded.

Peter nodded and then Hank expressed the thought that was racing through their minds.

"What the heck's going on, sir? They must have gained contact with *Rugged* as we passed through the Mona passage on the surface."

Peter whistled. "They are certainly organised — they must have a radar chain right out here."

Hank cocked his ear as the low *crrrump!* of a typical depth-charge pattern echoed across the bay.

"Poor old Number One. He's certainly having to learn fast."

Then they heard pattern after pattern exploding, and the beach trembled under them.

"I can't stand this, Hank. I can't bear listening to it. Let's press on to Platt's house. There's nothing we can do here and we may be disturbed by goofing parties coming down to watch the fun."

Peter found himself shaking when he slunk off into the scrub. Whether it was terror of the unknown and of the snakes that they might tread underfoot, or whether it was the sight of those destroyers giving *Rugged* the heat, he was not sure. Hank had taken the lead. Peter was in the middle, Bill bringing up the rear and Peter felt reassured to feel the burly seaman behind him. Then the depth-charging ceased abruptly. *Perhaps they've lost contact*, Peter thought hopefully, *or run out of charges*. But he was afraid of the hunters in the bay.

They watched the lamps coming on in the village that lay less than a mile away, yellow lights, dim and orange like Chinese lanterns. And like glow-worms, the pinpoints of light gradually studded the hillsides behind the village that sprawled round Road Harbour.

"Look, sir — yonder's the house." Peter heard Bill's deep voice behind him. "They're electric, surely, much brighter than the others."

They gazed up at the string of lights that suddenly twinkled halfway up the hillside, directly behind the pier that stretched like a finger into the bay which was now visible. Their brilliance traced the shape of a large hacienda-type bungalow. From Brown's description in Kingston, this must be Colonel Platt's place.

"Make for those lights, Hank."

The American waved his hand in acknowledgement. He started striding towards the line of shacks now appearing at the end of the rough track upon which they had just stumbled. As they approached the village an excitable hum could be heard near the pier.

"I reckon the whole town's turned out, Hank. Come on — no more concealment. We're three planters up from St. Vincent. We're thinking of settling here to try sea island cotton."

They strode towards the crowd which had now gathered in the road that ran along the edge of the bay. Hank stuffed his hands in his pockets and was enjoying kicking the coconut husks as he walked. Suddenly they were in the midst of the throng, and all around them was the smell of paraffin and the jabber of excited West Indian voices. The three friends eased their way through, until Hank saw a track running up towards the bungalow on the hill. They moved unobtrusively into the lane and then they were in the dark. The dust smelt dank under their feet and the leaves of the palms rustled above them. They suddenly felt hemmed in by the lush vegetation and they found themselves talking in whispers. A star shell was bursting in the bay and its reflection drifted eerily against the clouds to illuminate the foreshore.

"Halt a moment, Hank."

They stopped by a whitewashed wall and laid their plans.

"Hank, you lead, as you're trained to this sort of thing," Peter whispered. "I'll keep you covered and Bill can bring up the rear. I reckon this is the estate wall of Platt's bungalow and we'll go straight up to his front door through the drive, if we can find it."

They cocked their revolvers and started following the wall up the hill. They came at last to a portal set in the wall between two stone pillars. Hank pushed gently and the door swung on its hinges… Peter waited a few seconds and then he and Bill followed swiftly, Bill closing it after him.

They were in a beautifully kept garden with lawns like satin that ran down the slope to the sea. The tree frogs were croaking and a musty smell of dampness exuded from the ground. They could see the lights on the balcony but no sign of life.

"Wait here, Bill," Peter whispered. "Hank will cover me when I call at the front door. Maybe they're expecting us tonight."

Peter slipped past the tall American and approached the steps that led to the front door which stood open. Hank vanished behind a bank of hibiscus.

Peter walked straight up the steps. The wooden planks rang hollowly beneath his feet and then his head was above the level of the verandah. The front door was ajar and through the gap Peter could see a pleasantly furnished hall, rush mats lending a cool atmosphere to the open space. He walked boldly to the door and rang the bell. He felt his heart beating and suddenly he wanted to run. After he'd crossed the threshold there could be no turning back… As he was rehearsing the password, a barrage of star shell cascaded behind and below him in the bay. There was a triumphant *aaaah!* from the watching crowd and then a blood-curdling yell when the destroyers wheeled into the attack. Peter turned away his face.

"Come in!" a jovial voice shouted from inside. "Come along in and shut the mosquito door. I don't want to be eaten by the darned things."

Peter stepped inside. On his right was a half-open door, and the room beyond glowed with light. He pushed the door open and entered. A middle-aged man was sprawled in a chair facing him, his legs stretched out in front of him. He was holding a pair of horn-rimmed spectacles in one hand. He looked at Peter with amusement but the eyes were shrewd.

"And whom, sir, do I have the honour of addressing at this time of the morning?"

Peter stood still and then Colonel Platt rose.

"Cigar?" Peter asked, tendering his case.

The Colonel took a cigar and removed the band.

"I don't usually smoke in Lent," he said, and added, looking at the band, "But I smoke only Havanas."

Peter relaxed. "Jamaicans are just as good," he replied.

Platt smiled. He stepped forward and took Peter's hand.

"My God!" he exclaimed. "We thought you'd forgotten us. Have you anyone with you?" He moved over to the sideboard on which stood a whisky decanter.

Peter grunted and pointed outside.

"We came in *Rugged*, sir. She's being hunted at the moment. My two friends are waiting outside."

"Well, bring them in, for heaven's sake. They can't stay out there or they may get picked up. Bring 'em in." He went with Peter to the front door, his arm across the young man's shoulder. Peter beckoned in the darkness and they waited in the light for Hank and Bill. A few seconds later they were all inside the study and Colonel Platt was pouring out whiskies for them.

When their glasses were filled he faced them with a smile.

"May I say, gentlemen, how pleased I am to see you? We have been expecting you." His eyes moved to the door which had clicked behind the three visitors.

Peter turned round. Three bare-footed men stood behind them. Their eyes were expressionless and they held sub-machine guns in front of them.

"Don't do anything rash," a silky voice purred from the sideboard. "My men are itchy on the trigger. They'd prefer you dead than alive!"

CHAPTER 8

The Brainwash

The helicopter hovered for a moment above Tortola, checked its bearings, then swooped off down the string of islands on a southerly course. From his position in the tail, Hank could see nothing, but Peter and Bill could watch the scene unfolding below them.

In Tortola, the traitorous Platt had extracted nothing from them, in spite of locking them in different huts. Their guards had taken their money and knocked them about, but Platt soon saw that this method was too crude: better to send them to Dominica, the Party's Indoctrination Centre. And so, a day later, a helicopter from the school at Dominica landed with two of its own air police.

But now, as Peter gazed down upon the water that he had sailed in *Rugged* less than forty-eight hours ago, an overpowering hatred of the totalitarian system swept over him. Below them he could see the great sweep of islands curving to the southward, and upon their shores a thin ribbon of white broke lazily. The expanse of turquoise that lapped the chain of islands deepened to mauve, then became indigo to seaward. *Rugged* had sailed through this Caribbean less than two days ago and below them at this moment she might be lying, a broken, twisted thing, with all on board…

Peter felt his nails cutting into the palms of his hands: that brute Platt had delighted in reporting that the destroyers had sunk the nuclear.

"Bad news for you, I'm afraid," he'd said smarmily. "You might as well confess and join us now, you know, for two reasons."

Peter had ignored him, but the guard kicked him savagely to his feet. With irritation Platt had continued:

"Firstly, because you will submit eventually and you might as well avoid as much pain as possible."

Peter looked Platt straight in the eye and the traitor could not face the contempt. Stung to anger, the planter had struck him then.

"Secondly, you obstinate idiot, your submarine was sunk last night."

Peter was numbed by the news. His brain slowly thawed, but because of the exhaustion from lack of sleep and food, it was not until after Platt had left him that his true feelings welled to the surface.

And now once again the hate for these Communists raged through him. Nothing was sacred as long as they got their own way: murder, blackmail, lies, sedition, such were the stock-in-trade of these ruthless and unscrupulous fanatics. With supreme presumption, they'd infiltrate an area that had been tolerably happy; within a few months the wretched inhabitants would be betrayed, set against each other and rendered mad with discontent; and all in the name of freedom and democracy. What hypocrites!

Peter felt sick.

Platt had misread them greatly, even to the extent of thinking that the news of *Rugged*'s sinking would weaken them; instead their will had stiffened. Whether they would be able to withstand the indoctrination at Dominica was another matter. He hadn't got much out of Platt, but at least he'd gathered that the Bishop of the Antilles was connected somehow with the scheme of things. They would know soon enough.

For ten hours they watched the necklace of islands sliding beneath them. They flew over hundreds of islands, islands that brought back memories of happy, carefree days as a Snotty in *York*, the old flagship of the America and West Indies Station.

Dead Man's Chest Island where he had landed with the Boys' Division for a cricket match; Saba Island, rearing abruptly from the sea to nearly three thousand feet, a pinnacle of mystery. St. Kitts, the arcadian island that the delighted Christopher Columbus named after himself, where they had landed to refuel. Gazing down from the helicopter, he could see the lime groves, spattering the hillsides with green.

St. John's, the capital of Antigua, lay thirty miles away to the eastward just visible from their height. Hazy with distance, the island was important with its ancient town of St. John's, so named by Columbus after a church in Seville. English Harbour, the important sugar port, which once careened and refitted Nelson's fleet before setting out on the long chase that ended with Trafalgar. The old spars and cannonballs were still lying about the shipyard when *York* had visited the island before the war. The Punch Bowl and Mount Misery that they had just skirted when flying over St. Kitts; what history these names recalled!

Peter twisted on to his side. His bonds were cutting into his wrists. Hank and Bill were trying to snatch some sleep, but they had arranged secretly that one should always be awake. It was Peter's turn, but exhaustion made him drowsy. The guard faced him impassively, the tommy gun across his knees. The pilot was sitting above them, and the heat of the sun made the whole crew sleepy. From time to time the pilot with his high cheekbones looked down at his human cargo, but otherwise he displayed little interest. Even at Road Harbour, whilst waiting for his prisoners, he'd sat immobile while the crowd nearly lynched them. It had been a terrifying moment and Peter still shuddered at the memory. The West Indians had changed out of all recognition and were now thriving on hatred. They had rushed the guards at Tortola and tried to snatch the prisoners. As Peter was hustled into the helicopter, he'd heard the cry of the crowd, hungry for blood; and he'd seen the sign of The Serpent crudely painted on walls and clothing. Hysteria was in the air, terror and suspicion.

The engine of the helicopter suddenly dropped its revs, and when Peter peered through the port he saw the massive island of Dominica looming up on their port side. The helicopter was hovering now, and Peter had a chance to take in the grandeur of this beautiful island, queen of all the West Indies. The island rose perpendicularly from the sea, a massive hunk of mountain, towering nearly five thousand feet into the mists. The summit floated invisibly in the billowing clouds which encircled it, while at the foot of the mountains the brightest emerald green he'd ever seen enveloped the foothills. Peter gasped at the beauty of it and then the helicopter began to lose height. Down and down it fell until it landed with a lurch on the main square of Roseau, the capital townlet which takes its name from the valley lying behind it. A quay jutted from the rock, and they looked with wonder upon this miracle of nature that rose sheer from the sea.

They were jostled out of the helicopter, and then came the exquisite relief when the rotor fluttered to a stop. They were hustled at bayonet point to a waiting jeep. The few onlookers took little interest, for it was a monotonous event. Their guard still escorting them, they lay on the floor of the truck while it bounced out of the town and along the road which twisted up the sides of the foothills. The watchdog sat on the wheel box, and as soon as they were clear of the town, he allowed them to lean against the canvas sides. They looked over the bouncing tailboard and the road spun away dustily. The climb seemed unending, but when the engine finally stopped screaming as it sank into bottom gear, the scenery made them gasp. The jeep was boiling and when it reached the top the guard allowed them out to stretch their legs.

"You be here long time," he said, and grinned whilst he lit a cigarette. They sat on the parapet that ran the length of the road and looked down at the Roseau valley.

Peter had never seen anything like it. The transparency of the atmosphere made the sides of the Roseau mountain on the opposite side of the valley seem less than a hundred yards away. The hazy mauves and blues disappeared into the clouds where, they were told, a freshwater lake lay cupped in the summit. This phenomenon accounted for the string of waterfalls cascading down the sides of the mountain. The crystal water sparkled in the sunlight, its unattainable coolness tantalising beyond words as they watched the falls splashing down into the green of the lush valley that lay four thousand feet below.

The Roseau valley! The very name conjured up arcadian fantasies in their minds. The Rose valley: it was here that a famous lime juice company had grown its limes, and their plantations covered the valley bed. The silver ribbon of a river wound between the groves, and the sunlight flashed in the broken water, dazzling the onlookers on the perimeter road that led to the head of the valley. The Roseau valley! The devil had a foothold here, for the Indoctrination Centre lay at the head of the valley, hidden from the outside world and down amongst the groves.

The radiator had cooled, and they continued their journey along the crest of the eastern side of the valley until they reached the far end. The road suddenly dipped over the edge, and after a terrifying drive down a cleft in the side of the valley they lurched to a halt by a group of palms. They heard a gate swinging open ahead of them; the jeep whined into life, and when it crawled ahead they saw a high wire fence behind them with white coconut insulators interspersed along its length. By the swinging pole that constituted the barrier, there swaggered a sentry complete with tommy gun. An officer in khaki shorts and shirt stood next to him, and he had the high cheekbones of a Tartar. Peter's heart sank when they were bundled out and taken to the registration office.

They were frisked and made to strip and change into clean overalls. They were each given a number and then they were taken to the separate huts which ran along the edge of the groves, but inside the electrified fence. Peter was surprised to see so many West Indian planters about the place, as well as several Europeans. He was thrown into a stifling hut and told that the Commandant would see him shortly.

Peter felt the bonds on his wrists being removed and then there was darkness as the door creaked and shut. He licked his parched lips and rolled on to his back.

"Might as well get some sleep while I can," he muttered. "Never know when I'll get any more."

The softening-up treatment started that night. Each man was in a separate hut and each suffered the agony of not knowing the fate of the others. For two days, when the temperature inside the corrugated iron roof became intolerable, the prisoners roasted in solitude; for two nights they rolled and twisted on the dirt floor, trying to sleep. Although they could not have slept because of the discomfort, they were balked mainly by a large police light that came on at dusk, the huts becoming as bright as day. Each of them, unknown to the others, tried to smash the lights, but this proved impossible because of the strong glass and the wide grille in which they were fitted. A greasy tin of water and two limes were pushed through the door in the morning, and this banquet made up the day's ration.

On the evening of the third day Peter was lugged to his feet by a huge jailer. The door was thrown open and Peter was dragged into the sunlight. He stood blinking and swaying in the sudden brightness and, quickly collecting his senses, he turned towards his guard. But the man was striding towards the next hut, and a few seconds later Peter saw Bill Hawkins come staggering out. A hundred yards farther down, a tall American tottered from his tin shack and stood blinking beneath a group of palms. Peter shouted and his voice was strange and cracked. To their amazement they found themselves left alone, and their surprise was complete when they discovered they were allowed to roam through the beautiful grove.

"Like Southend holiday camp, sir," Bill grunted, grinning hugely.

"Listen, you two," Peter muttered. "I've a hunch they're going to try and soften us up now with pleasantries. Don't give anything away, but act 'wet'. We'll know their game soon enough, but of one thing you can be quite certain..."

"Uh-huh?" Hank grunted.

"These birds are experts at brainwashing and they know what they're doing. They aim to turn us into Commies. Remember George Blake?"

"Way back in the sixties?" Hank muttered. "Yes, I remember him. But he was notorious only because he was the first of thousands more like him. You Limeys even began to sympathise with them, remember?"

"Giddy optimists!" Bill swore. "Hullo! What's this?"

The path led between two clumps of limes, and they came upon a low-pitched building nestling beneath the shade of a group of palms. They stopped in their tracks as a group of Europeans by the steps turned to watch them. The leaves of the palms rustled above them in the silence.

"Come on, boys! Come and join us!"

Peter looked down at his hands and his clothes and shook his head. He and his friends were filthy.

An elderly planter strolled towards him, extending his hand.

"My name's Patterson, Harry Patterson," he boomed. "Come on in and get cleaned up. Have these idiotic guards forgotten about you?"

"Yes, they have." Hank swore violently.

Patterson shook his head. The guards were a forgetful lot: they'd done the same to him.

"Well, forget it now, boys. You'll feel better when you've freshened up. There're clean clothes for everyone in the shower room."

Half an hour later the three friends had changed. They were ravenously hungry but they felt clean and refreshed. They left their old clothes in the changing rooms and rejoined the group of men gathered outside the verandah of the Mess Hall.

"Planter's punch, sah?"

A waiter in a spotless apron purred in his ear. The drink looked delicious, the glass furred on the outside by the ice, and with the elusive smell of rum. The three men held out their hands eagerly.

"Cheers!" a jovial voice toasted. "Hope you enjoy your stay."

They were surrounded by a circle of inquisitive inmates of the camp. They all seemed to be content with life and were normal citizens: planters, merchants and shopkeepers, Peter thought. He couldn't believe the contrast of the present moment with their existence of the five previous days.

"Cheers!"

"Cheers! Skol! Bung-ho!" the greetings welcomed them. "Down the spout!"

The aperitifs slipped down too easily, and it wasn't long before the ice alone lay tinkling at the bottom of the glass, a slice of lime and the black pips of guava the only trace of an irresistible drink.

A shadow had brushed past Peter's shoulder and the waiter had poured him another punch. Peter grinned. This was going to be a good evening; he wasn't paying for it. He watched with amusement Hank's outstretched arm and then Bill longingly watching the tilted jug.

Peter felt a man on the opposite side of the circle watching him. Their eyes met for an instant before the stranger turned away. But in that second Peter had detected a gleam of satisfaction. The man turned and started to talk to his neighbour. From his profile, Peter judged him to be a European of eastern origin. And Peter sensed their peril.

They had eaten little for days. They were exhausted and they were thirsty. With a little alcohol their tongues would loosen amongst this friendly company, and if they were separated from each other they could be persuaded to talk. This was more dangerous than crude, physical torture. He tilted his glass and pretended to sip. He slipped across to Hank, and while conversing inanely with another guest, he managed to whisper his warning.

"Stop drinking. Tell Bill."

Peter lifted his glass again to his lips.

Hank nodded and lowered his arm. The glass tilted in his hand, and the precious liquid trickled to the green lawn on which they were standing.

"Dinner is served!"

Bill Hawkins looked at his Captain and grinned. This was a bit of 'orl right' and he didn't mind how far it went.

"Watch your step at dinner, Bill," Peter whispered. "Don't drink."

Bill winked. He was busy pouring his drink down the trouser leg of a planter who was waiting to ease through the congested door.

And then they found themselves separated. Hank was taken off by Patterson to one end of the long table, Bill to the other, with a sinister eastern European, while Peter was placed in the middle between two planters, one middle-aged, the other about his own vintage. Mr. President mumbled a few words at the head of the table, the guests raised clenched fists and they all sat down to what was to prove a memorable dinner.

A tantalising array of wine glasses and the gleaming rows of cutlery were almost too much for them after their privations, and they had to remind themselves of the game they were playing. The soup came and went and Peter's neighbours introduced themselves. The younger man, Jack Plowden, was a lecturer at the English College in Port of Spain. The elder merchant on his left went by the name of Tarisku, an oily character who cut no ice with Peter.

"When d'you come in?" Plowden asked. "I never saw your arrival."

Peter put down his soup spoon and tried to look the young man directly in the face. But Plowden was busy with the remnants of his soup and did not look up. With gingery hair, a hatchet-shaped face and with fair eyebrows that were almost invisible, Peter was not greatly taken by him. A foxy type…

"Three days ago," Peter replied. "These swine locked us in the pens and left us to rot."

"You're lucky. Some of 'em stay there for weeks before graduating."

"What d'you mean?"

The soup plates disappeared, and a slab of rock cod, dressed with a pink sauce that lay stickily across the top, appeared in front of Peter. He disliked rock cod.

"I should eat it up, old boy," Plowden grinned, whispering under his breath. "I've had some of this solitary confinement and starvation and I know what's good for me. Annoy them, and you're back in the pens… And drink up! They'll fill 'em up again."

Peter was beginning to dislike the fellow. But he seemed talkative and Peter wanted information.

"Where do we sleep tonight?"

"In the pens. Unless…"

Foxy turned towards Peter and the watery eyes met his momentarily. "Unless you see sense and decide to string along with us."

"What d'you mean by that?" Peter was on his guard and an edge had crept into his voice.

"Learn to co-operate with your hosts. After all, they're not doing you too badly, are they?"

Peter curled up inside. For a mess of pottage the man was selling his soul.

"No, not too badly. But I hate rock cod!" Peter let the man talk.

Plowden put down his knife and fork and folded his arms.

"Eat up, Sinclair, the Direktor's watching you. He doesn't like discourtesy."

"Oh, he doesn't, does he?" Peter laughed aloud.

What an insane world he'd suddenly entered! He felt he was in the nursery, and the unreality of the situation was absurd.

"Well, you can tell him to stuff it up his jumper!" Peter shoved the plate, complete with its cod, straight into the centre of the table. The wine glasses crashed and a thin rivulet of golden liquid trickled across the table. He'd upset his wine.

There was a shocked silence while Peter glared at the accusing glances which were directed at him. He grinned at the black-haired oaf who sat at the head, his hand halfway to his mouth, a crust of bread clutched between his podgy fingers. He looked like a toad and his eyes were gleaming in the bright light. He nodded at the waiter who stood behind Peter.

The mess was mopped up and the buzz of conversation resumed. Peter saw Hank and Bill smiling broadly and they exchanged winks. They'd taken the hint and neither had touched their wine.

"And," Peter continued, "how d'you know my name?"

Plowden toyed for a second with his bread before replying. He waited while the entrée, roast quail and sweet potatoes, was put in front of him and then he stared at Peter's place which remained empty.

"You'll excuse us if we start?" Plowden asked. "You won't be given any food now. You're in disgrace."

"Go ahead," Peter laughed. "This is priceless! But how d'you get my name?" he insisted.

"News travels fast in these islands. We always know who's coming, sometimes days in advance. The authorities tell us to look after any new guests."

Peter swallowed. He wanted to hit this fellow.

"If you learnt to co-operate, you know," Plowden continued, "you'd get on much better. After all, what's the point of making yourself miserable for so long, when you're bound to submit in the end? You know capitalism is doomed anyhow, so you might as well join us now. We demand little of you."

Peter glued his eyes to his empty place. They were coming to the point at last.

"Well, what do you traitors want of us?"

The question was like a pistol shot. Plowden swallowed, and when he had finished his mouthful he turned to Peter with a smile.

"You're the traitor, my dear fellow. You're the enemy of freedom, people like you. You let the Americans do what they like with you." Plowden's voice became shriller. This was a sore point with him and men always become angry when they are least sure of their motives. "The Americans and the Roman Catholics are the greatest barriers to democracy."

Peter was enjoying this claptrap. They talked the same nonsense the world over! The terrifying thing was that they actually believed the stuff, whatever the facts…

"Look at this Bishop of the Antilles. He's right up to his neck in it."

Peter pricked up his ears. The Bishop…?

"But he's an Anglican, surely? And a wonderful fellow, I'm told. Haven't you devils locked him up?"

Plowden glanced at Peter with pity.

"Drink up, old chap," he said. "Let's not argue. You'll need my friendship before you've finished, if you go on like this."

There was a crash at the far end of the table and a scraping of cutlery. Hank was pushing back his chair, and a quail was slipping from the bald pate of his next-door neighbour. A brown smear of gravy trickled slowly down the forehead and into the man's eyes.

"Hooray! Hurray for *Rugged*!" Bill exploded as he pushed his chair back, too, and then they were bundled from the room. Peter heard Plowden bidding him "*au revoir*" and he found himself catapulted into the darkness.

"Oh, you naughty boys!" Peter shouted as they were being hustled to their cells. "You naughty, naughty boys!"

The next seven days were almost unbearable. Short of physical torture, they underwent their separate hells, each in his own corrugated hut. Deprived of sleep by day and night, grilled by inhuman interrogators, starved and humiliated in front of their janitors and parched with thirst during the sweltering days, they found at last what their captors wanted.

"Why did you come to the West Indies?"

Peter stood between two guards and he was swaying so that they had to support him. It was three in the morning and he'd been grilled since eleven-thirty. The swine who sat facing him had chain-smoked and the air was foul in the cell of the interrogation block.

"You came to spy, didn't you? You had secret instructions for the Bishop of the Antilles."

Peter had heard the same insistent question from somewhere, long ago. He'd heard it remorselessly for longer than he could remember and he felt his mind slipping, he was so tired. *Tell them anything, for God's sake. It was extracted under duress anyway, so didn't count…*

"All you have to do, you know, is to sign here…"

Peter heard the persuasive voice crooning silkily. The blinking light above him hurt his eyes. He wondered how Hank and Bill were getting on under all this … only one of them had to weaken for a moment and the enemy had won. He remembered the martyrs behind the Iron Curtain, dragged before their persecutors, and spouting confessions like trained dogs… Cardinal Mindszenty, President Benes, Imre Nagy, the Hungarian martyrs, and the thousands who had resisted but who were forgotten by the civilised world. They all resisted, but some had mouthed their 'confessions' before the end. There was a limit to what the human mind could bear. He'd never forget that photograph of Cardinal Mindszenty…

"Sign here, plees."

Hank and Bill…? Were they holding out? And suddenly his brain cleared for a second. The reality of the situation flashed through his mind and he took strength in the fortitude of his friends who were suffering near him. Peter wasn't going to be the first to crack. He squared his shoulders.

"Sign here, plees. You can rejoin our community then, Sinclair. Food, drink, clean clothes, freedom…"

Peter could see the laden table, taste the cool, sparkling wine, feel the freshness of crisp, white, laundered clothes…

"Take him away."

They flung him back into his cell, where he crouched trembling, unable to lie down for lack of space. He tried to sleep on his feet, but each time that his eyes closed his knees would buckle and he'd regain half-consciousness by banging his head against the sides of the hut. The ghastly night dragged by and then the whole process was repeated. Scorching heat, unconsciousness, a burning thirst, and the terror of the coming night… Peter felt his mind slipping and he wondered how long he could withstand this; and every time it was the thought of Hank and Bill which saved him.

That evening, the door suddenly flung open and his tormentor stood straddled in the rays of the setting sun. He looked down on the filthy figure of the Englishman. He was smiling.

"Better get cleaned up, Sinclair. The Direktor wants you and your friends to dine with us again." He turned on his heel and Peter saw him striding towards the huts of Hank and Bill... At least they must be alive.

Peter held on to the wall of the hut while he recovered himself. A shower, clean clothes, decent food and something to drink... He shivered as he let the sunlight soak into him. He mustn't weaken, mustn't give in, but how his tormentors knew their job! They knew just when to stop, when their 'patients' were on the brink of insanity: a gibbering madman was useless to them. Then the contrast of gracious living could prove the last straw. He summoned his willpower and swayed towards the shower rooms. Hank and Bill soon joined him and they were in the same state. They smiled at each other, but from their eyes Peter knew they'd held out. They knew it without speaking.

"What did the swine want you to sign, sir?" Bill asked, as he let the cleansing water drench him. They couldn't be heard by the guards at the doorway.

"Oh, the usual guff! That I accept their creed, that I came here to spy, that the Bishop of the Antilles is an accomplice, etcetera, etcetera..."

"Same with me, sir," Hank added, "but I've discovered where they've got the Bishop. They've locked him up somewhere in Trinidad. I gather there's a big day coming. Some sort of rebellion, a sort of 'D'-day."

"Let's bust all this up tonight, if they give us the same affair as they did last time," Peter said. "I'm fed up with the devils."

"So'm I, sir. Particularly those so-called intellectuals," Bill grinned. "Come on, sir, let's chamfer them up!"

The drenching of the showers drowned the whispers of the three conspirators.

Plowden met Peter outside the Mess Hall as if nothing had happened. Five days and nights had elapsed, a period in which the fellow traveller must have known the agonies through which the three men were passing. Peter wanted to punch the hypocrite squarely on the nose; these people were so expert at sticking up for everyone else but their own country. Ugh!

"How nice to see you, Sinclair; good to have you back. Have a drink?"

"Thanks." Peter smiled to himself. Might as well make the most of the evening while they could.

"Hope you've changed your mind, Sinclair. Your friend Jefferson tells me he's considering it. After all, you don't really believe the tosh you're led to believe in England, do you?"

"I've been thinking, too. Cheers!"

"Big Business leads you by the ears, hoodwinks the lot of us. You believe anything the Press lords give you, don't you?"

The tree frogs were croaking in the groves. The evening breeze was swaying the palms, and Peter revelled in the cool of the night. How exquisite it was! He hardly heard Plowden, but realised only just in time that the earnest idiot was still spouting. After all, look at his mouth! It still opened and shut, but behind his rimless glasses the eyes of a fanatic gleamed.

"Don't you, Sinclair?"

"Yes, I suppose so…"

"But it's all lies, lies, d'you hear, lies…"

What's he getting so excited about? thought Peter, and he was relieved to see that the crowd outside the verandah was moving in to dinner. He wanted food now, more than anything else in the world. With food inside him, he could resist anything again. He joined the queue and left Plowden.

Peter was shown to his place, but to his chagrin Plowden was again placed on his right. As the Englishman stood behind his chair he felt the President's eye on him and the back of his neck prickled. He looked up and, sure enough, the toad-like figure was watching him intently. He looked away as Peter stared back.

When they were all packed round the white napery, they stood for a moment while Mr. Toad went through the ritual of a Marxist grace. They raised their right fists and then there was a rumble of chairs as they sat down. Bill beat the field and was waiting for the soup before the first diner had even drawn back his chair.

"I expect you're hungry?"

The question came from the merchant on Peter's left, Tarisku, the man who had sat next to him before.

"Not too bad, really."

Peter found his hand trembling when he lifted the soup spoon. If he hadn't wanted the food so much, he'd have hurled it in these traitors' faces. *Here they were — turncoats who'd been British subjects for years, deliberately betraying the country that had nurtured them. No wonder the Old Country had gone downhill! They were typical of the woolly thinkers who insidiously spread their rotten ideas all over the British Isles; no one minded, no one cared… We were paying for it now all right. Look at Plowden, a typical end product of some fellow travelling renegade…*

The soup trickled down Peter's throat and he felt his stomach assimilating the sustenance. He longed to yell, to scream at the top of his voice, and he felt himself trembling as he held himself in check. His eyelids drooped with weariness, and by the time the main dish had arrived it was all he could do to keep his eyes open. The drone of Plowden's voice drifted into his semi-consciousness. What claptrap the little man spouted, what unmitigated drivel! If only he'd dry up for just one moment…

He remembered getting through the cheese and biscuits and then he heard the chairs being dragged back. The meal was over, he'd be taken back to the hut, he supposed … and then he rebelled and his mind cleared suddenly. He looked at Hank who was smiling, at Bill who winked. Ah, yes! This was the moment they'd been waiting for…

Mr. Toad was mouthing platitudes at the head of the table, and then the clenched fists were raised once more. All eyes were upon Mr. Toad so they missed the next development.

"Diving Stations!"

The clarion call came from Peter, defiant and strong. The diners turned abruptly towards the shout, but they only saw three gaps in the places round the table. The tall American had heaved his wine glass at Mr. President but it had missed. It shattered against the back wall. A purple stain was trickling down the plaster…

Then something extraordinary took place: the table suddenly upped and started moving towards the other end of the room. The diners watched the tablecloth and all the fittings go waltzing past them, like the pantomime horse on a stage, all lumps and bumps. And from underneath came laughter, loud, derisory guffaws, punctuated by somewhat rude observations upon the guests and their creed in general. Chaos reigned. It was three minutes before order was restored. The culprits were extracted from beneath the collapsing table but not before they had managed to drag the tablecloth after them. The whole dinner, food, glasses, cutlery, everything crashed to the floor. It was a glorious shambles.

Peter, Hank and Bill were speechless as they struggled with the guards who had been summoned. How grand it had been, all their pent-up emotion suddenly released! They laughed in the face of Mr. Toad who stood in front of them, his eyes cold and expressionless.

"You will regret this, you fools. You are no longer any use to us here. You won't co-operate, so I must send you elsewhere." His little eyes gleamed wickedly as he fought for self-control. "You will fly to Castries tomorrow, our Security Police Headquarters in St. Lucia. We shall see what Colonel Yakov can do. You'll regret that you didn't accept my hospitality, my friends."

He swung on his heel to return to the Mess Hall. The tree frogs were croaking in the night outside, and in the darkness above them the palm leaves rustled.

CHAPTER 9

Nightmare World

The helicopter took off at dawn the next morning. It climbed from the Roseau valley, and looking back at the deceptive beauty, the three prisoners were not sorry to see the island disappear. If they were to be tortured again, they might as well have a change of scene… They consoled themselves by such rationalisation and kept up each other's spirits by baiting their coloured guards. Martinique, the French island and the largest and northernmost of the Windwards, passed slowly beneath them. Right ahead, a mountain summit rose from the ocean: it was the peak of Pigeon Island which guarded the northern tip of the island of St. Lucia. From this eyrie, Admiral Rodney watched the French fleet putting to sea from Port de France in Martinique. The blue mountain slipped down their port side and then below them they saw Gros Islet Bay. Rodney slipped from here in April, 1782, to break the French line at the Battle of the Saints, the first time this manoeuvre had been carried out. It was to be developed by Lord Nelson at Trafalgar, twenty-three years later.

A green range of mountains stretched far into the distance and then a yellow strip of sandy beach appeared below them. Peter could see the white ribbon of surf breaking lazily upon the shore, and when they lost height he could see the palms waving along the edge of the sand.

Port Castries, the capital of St. Lucia, lay at the head of the bay, a harbour nibbled from the coastline. They flew over a capacious stone barracks which straddled the low-lying westerly arm of the bay. Once the Vigie Country Club, but now the Federation Headquarters of the Security Police, it was originally the barracks for British troops when France was fighting England. Three thousand soldiers, killed by yellow fever, lay in their graves beneath the walls of this inhospitable building. Although during the first thirty years of the twentieth century there was considerable waste of life through cholera, smallpox and yellow fever, today there is little disease.

The helicopter started to lose height over the wooded mountains, and for once the guard broke silence. With vivid gesticulations he explained that these forests were the home of the second most deadly snake in the world; here lived the fer-de-lance, the reptile that struck like forked lightning. Peter shuddered as he watched the fear in the man's face. His eyes were gleaming as he described the snake, and Peter couldn't understand the terror which the mention of it had produced.

They flew over a gash in the mountain side and then crossed a valley which was filled by a mound. Here, the guard explained, the side of the mountain had slipped. It slid across the valley, killing one hundred and thirteen workmen at Christmas time in 1938. In its history, the island of St. Lucia, because of its central geographical position, had suffered more than most: it was too valuable.

The helicopter swooped low over the palm-fringed beach, a gigantic dragonfly, hovering a moment before dunking on to the sand. They jumped out and were hustled through this helicopter park at the edge of the palms. A waiting jeep trundled down the dirt road and five minutes later they drove through the portals of the Headquarters of the Security Police. A massive door swung behind them and they were within the fortress. They were escorted down a flight of stone steps and flung into the old dungeons. They lay in the darkness listening to the scampering of rats in the straw.

Whether it was intentional or not Peter never found out, but they were all incarcerated together. Lying there in the filth, in the heat and stench of the sweltering humidity, they soon realised that Dominica had been a picnic compared to what was coming to them. It was on his first interrogation that Peter discovered this.

He was frogmarched to the Interrogating Cell at eleven thirty at night. He winced when he saw the room: lights that scalded his eyes by their brightness, no ventilation; and strange devices protruding from the walls. The essential equipment of a totalitarian state, in fact, and he took strength in his freedom. They weren't going to win, he'd never give in, even if they used these instruments of torture, curse their rotten methods… The door clanged behind him. The two guards stepped back while he faced his interrogator.

Peter was surprised to see that the man was a civilian. A cigarette drooped from his lips and the smoke curled upwards across his eyes, half choking him. He lifted his eyebrows continually to avoid the smoke. He was a little man, quite inconspicuous, a civil servant: reliable and conscientious, but an ambitious man, Peter judged, and ruthless. A fanatic with no soul.

On the desk was a name indicator, like a bank clerk's: Mr. Cronin. *Mr. Cronin*, Peter thought grimly; *Mr. Cronin of the Murder Squad! Mr. Cronin, Qualified Practitioner for Extracting Confessions, efficient in every way, never known to fail. What a lot these Commies were!* And he squared his shoulders to face his ordeal.

"Ah, Mr. Sinclair, we've been expecting you," the man said. "I have had an Advice Note about you and your — ah —

friends. Number 061007, I believe," and he started to thumb through his files.

"Lieutenant, please," Peter snapped. "Lieutenant Peter Sinclair, of the Royal Navy, and you'll remember that."

The high-cheekboned interrogator rose from behind the desk and approached his prisoner. There was a *crack!* and Peter reeled from the blow that stung him across the cheek. The guards held him as he staggered.

"Don't do that again," Peter said.

Two more blows rang crisply, and Peter felt blood oozing from his mouth.

"You must realise, *Mister* Sinclair, I'll do as I please. For once in your sweet life you'll take orders from someone you consider inferior, and you'll obey everyone, d'you understand?" Cronin nodded at one of the guards.

"You're entitled to ask for my name, rank and number only," Peter muttered grimly. "You'll get no more."

Cronin's tone changed to a wheedling persuasiveness.

"Why don't you and your friends give in? You know, old chap, you're all convinced eventually, it's only a matter of time and of er … pain. It seems such a waste to endure all that and yet reach the same result in the end."

"What do you want us to do?"

"Well, it's too foolish for words — merely to put your name to a document."

Peter saw his chance. "Let me see it first."

"First?" Cronin asked hopefully. "I'm afraid the Direktor has it."

"I won't sign anything without reading it first."

"Of course, old boy, any sensible chap would do that. But the Direktor won't be back until this evening and he has instructed me to take you all down to the town. The Serpent King is holding his last meeting before moving on."

"Why are you taking us there?"

Cronin laughed shortly.

"To convince you three that you are wasting your time if you refuse to sign the confessions. You'll see how the natives feel; how solidly they are behind The King. They mean to have their freedom and want their own people to govern them."

"So you're helping them?" Peter laughed bitterly. "But what are you asking us to confess? That we're terribly sorry; we've made a ghastly mistake and really love you Commies?"

"No," Cronin replied shortly. "It's simple, really. There are three main statements: that you landed from your submarine to spy; that you came to contact the Bishop of the Antilles who is involved with the spy ring; that you accept Communism and renounce your Christian creed. Nothing in it really. Just a few typewritten lines. They mean little to you because you don't have to believe what you've signed. It's under duress, isn't it?"

Peter was trembling. How easy it all seemed. After all, what did an enforced signature mean? It held no validity in law. He looked up and saw Cronin smiling.

These kid-glove methods were working, Cronin thought. *It was only a matter of time; when this fellow saw the hysteria of the mob he'd realise there was no point in further resistance. He'd concentrate on Sinclair: the others would follow.*

"Where's the Bishop?" Peter asked curtly.

Cronin paused. "Why do you want to know?"

"I'd like to talk to him: and besides, I shan't sign anything unless I know that the Bishop is alive. That's why."

"He's in Trinidad." There could be no harm; he was sharing a confidence with an equal.

"Is he alive?"

"Yes, of course! You don't think we still behave like that, do you?" The little man spread his hands wide and his eyes opened innocently. "And besides…"

"Besides what?"

"He's wanted for the final rally."

"Why?"

"He's our star turn, of course. He will have to be in at…"

"… the death?" Peter snapped.

"No, old boy, of course not. You seem to think we are uncivilised, crude murderers, without thought for justice. We don't work that way any more. We get what we want by more refined methods."

"Of course," Peter answered. "But when's the final rally before the uprising? Presumably you'll take over the whole Federation?"

"It's in our grasp already. We've chosen Commonwealth Day to put the seal on it. We thought you'd all appreciate the irony of it. I must say The King thinks it amusing." Cronin lit another cigarette. "But come and see for yourself. I can spare the afternoon from this dreadful place and the Direktor won't be back until the evening. I'll be your guide in Castries."

He motioned to the guards to take the prisoner away, and his ferrety eyes were gleaming. "See you in the town. I can't travel with you — somewhat undignified."

Peter understood why Cronin refused to travel with them when, at half past two, they were thrown into a jeep. They blinked in the sunlight, and before they knew it they were bumping along the dirt road, a wire grille covering the back of the vehicle. An armed guard with a red armband sat next to each prisoner; they looked sadistic brutes, probably specially selected. They grinned at their prisoners as they lit up the cigarettes which smelt like Caporals. The stink reminded Peter of his Chaser days when he worked in the Channel with the Free French.

They drove past the flat expanse of the old tennis courts which was now the Direktor's private helicopter park. They bumped between the palm groves until they reached Castries, capital of St. Lucia. Silent humanity was streaming into the port, women and children too. They wore their brightest colours, but they seemed strangely silent for a West Indian crowd. The women kept their eyes on their shuffling feet, and the men looked furtive, not meeting each other's glances. *Something strange going on*, thought Peter. *The Serpent King must have a strong hold over them, because they were unnaturally cowed.*

The square opened out before them, and the jeep nudged its way through the crowd until it was forced to stop. In the centre of the area was a raised platform upon which stood a table with a stand on it. From this hung a heavy golden belt, shining in the sun. Great rubies and emeralds glowed from the gold, and the crowd was gazing on it almost in adoration. Peter felt the hysteria that lay beneath the surface, and he felt sick when he saw the hate that was directed upon them as they waited in the jeep. A clod of dirt splattered against the grille and he heard coarse laughter. Their guards didn't relish acting as targets so they quit the back of the jeep. They stood back and directed the aim, jeering and laughing uproariously.

"Turn round!" Peter shouted above the hubbub.

They stood back to back and faced the mob. They avoided most of the offensive missiles, but by the time the crowd had lost interest they were in a filthy condition from the rotten fruit and vegetables that had spattered against the grille.

Until the Tortola incident, Peter had never seen a crowd full of hate. These people, men, women and children, were in the grip of an elemental terror. Not only were they starving, but from their furtive faces, which were usually so open and happy, there emanated an atmosphere of mistrust and hate. They were waiting for something and they meant to have their way. From the animal baying that came from the younger men, they were in a dangerous mood.

Peter saw a group of them advancing on the jeep. One carried a petrol tin and by the howls of encouragement from the onlookers their intention was obvious.

"Get them out, Sergeant."

Peter heard Cronin's voice below him as the first youth drenched the truck with petrol. There was a fumbling with the padlock and the three captives bundled out as the jeep exploded in a sheet of flame. They felt the heat singeing their clothes and they hurled themselves to the ground to roll out any flame. There was a howl of delight from the far edges of the crowd, but this soon turned to anger when they saw that they had been balked. Then, as Cronin hustled them towards a side street, protected on the flanks by the frightened guards, the crowd roared and then, like a small child who loses interest in his new toy, it turned about to face the new attraction.

"We're all right now: the Serpent King's arrived. You'd better watch this to see what I mean."

The crowd had thinned here, and as they reached the alleyway Peter felt his guard lurching against him. They both tripped and fell and in the commotion he heard Cronin cursing. Bill had fallen deliberately to the ground, and in the tangle of limbs Hank had suddenly bolted. He was lost in the crowd already, and although one guard went after him, the man soon returned baffled and confused.

Cronin was livid. He'd lost one of his prisoners and he'd have to face the Direktor. He'd better return to Headquarters, even without transport. The jeep was a burnt-out wreck, and it would be a risky business escorting these two through the crowd. Better ring up.

"Sergeant, leave your prisoner and go and phone for transport. I'll take care of this one," and a snub-nosed automatic was pressed into the small of Peter's back. "Hurry up, Sergeant."

Peter and Bill were grinning at Cronin's discomfiture. The little runt was sweating with fear and muttering beneath his breath.

"You'll regret that escape," he hissed. "Yakov'll make you two pay for it." He dug the barrel deeper into Peter's flesh.

While they waited, they watched the hubbub on the platform. An enormous figure was addressing the crowd. Resplendent in his flashing jewels and wearing the mantle of kingship with a natural dignity, he looked magnificent. His bass voice was rumbling around the square and when he spoke the crowd hung on his every word. Softly he reminded them of their ancestry, of their forebears who had been here centuries before Columbus; of the proud Caribs, the rightful inheritors of these islands, and how they had been exploited for three hundred years by the white settler. Gradually, skilfully, he hypnotised them by his oratory. Then his voice boomed more rapidly and with mounting excitement as he outlined the destiny that lay ahead of them. He was shouting now, and suddenly there was an hysterical edge to his voice which made Peter shudder. The King was gesticulating now and he pointed to the Sacred Belt which was flashing in the sun.

A man yelled from below the platform and the demand was quickly taken up by the mob. They had come a long way for this and didn't intend to be cheated.

"When he puts on the Belt," Cronin explained excitedly, "it's the signal for human sacrifice."

"Evidently that's what the crowd wants," Peter answered. "What form does it take?"

"You'll soon see. Watch carefully. They usually use the snakes." Cronin nodded at the black crate that stood at the back of the platform. "Fer-de-lance," he said. "A deadly reptile! There is the added advantage of prolonging the entertainment because the snake plays with its victim — like a cat with a mouse, you know." The tip of his tongue licked his thin red lips. "The Sacred Belt is a replica of the fer-de-lance. They leave it on view during the daytime."

"What happens to it at night? Surely it's valuable and would be stolen?" Peter asked.

"They wouldn't dare. The natives believe the beastly thing has supernatural powers. But at night it's locked up. They put it in that casket and bring it to Headquarters for safekeeping." Cronin shuddered. Even he felt the miasma of the terror that had gripped men's minds.

The King turned towards the shining Belt. The crowd squealed expectantly. Who was to be the victim? They looked towards the wrecked jeep, and then someone spotted Cronin and his protégés. A howl rose from the square and there was a surge towards the white men.

"It looks as if you're up against it, too," Peter said grimly to Cronin. "You'd better think fast. Don't move or they'll rush us."

Then above the noise there was a stentorian bellow. The King was addressing them again, and his power was such that he commanded immediate silence.

"Fools!" he cried. "Don't waste time on this white trash! We can claim them at any time. I came here today, not to wear the

Sacred Belt, but to prepare you for the greatest of all days: the Day of Freedom, my comrades!" The cheers rang around the square, and the mass of people halted, mesmerised by their speaker. It was terrifying to feel that the crowd, which was being mesmerised into this ugly trance, was typical of the whole Federation. They were following the Serpent King to hell, and shamefully they revelled in the process.

"Wear the Belt, O King!" they cried in a frenzy. "The Sacred Belt, wear the Belt! We want sacrifice!"

At this moment, there was the whine of an engine at the bottom of the alleyway, and Cronin started to run towards it. As Peter turned to follow, he saw the King seize the Golden Belt. The crowd gasped in anticipation and suddenly there was silence — perhaps they'd persuaded their King?

"I will wear this on Commonwealth Day, my people! We will rise as one on that day, our Liberation Day. And then your sacrifice shall be the one you hate above all others…"

"Now! Give us sacrifice now!" the crowd yelled as it stamped in the dirt. Then a shrill voice piped from the front ranks:

"Who will it be, O King? Is he worth waiting for?"

"That traitor, the Bishop of the Antilles will be our sacrifice for Freedom Day!" The crowd hushed, bewildered and shocked. "A ship will be coming to take as many as possible down to Trinidad where the last rally will be taking place on the eve of Commonwealth Day," he continued, and the enormous man spat in contempt at the words. He carefully replaced the shining belt in the casket, and, as Peter reached the jeep, he could still hear the drone of the man's words.

As Bill and he leapt into the back, he watched the officer who was sitting in the passenger seat lean across to talk to Cronin, who stood by the door, one hand on the handle.

"Colonel Yakov is back," he was saying. "He is waiting for you."

Cronin stood still for a second and then he leapt into the back, to be among his charges. He was terrified of the Colonel at the best of times, and now he'd lost one of his prisoners. The jeep shot off at full speed, bumping and lurching as it tore round the corners, driven at furious speed by its native driver.

"Why did you bring us to see all this?" Peter asked Cronin. "You could have told us about it."

Cronin turned towards Peter.

"We want you to realise the futility of your position," he said, his eyes full of hate. "We're bound to win in the end."

"Maybe. But you've convinced me about the native population. It's in an explosive mood. But you won't get *us* to change."

"You fool, Sinclair!" the little man hissed. "After the Colonel has finished with you, you'll wish that you'd never been born."

CHAPTER 10

The Colonel

They left Peter and Bill for a week in the dungeons. They were separated now, so neither had the opportunity of seeing whether the other was holding out against 'The Treatment'. On returning from Castries on the day of the Serpent King's visit, it was Cronin who had been summoned by Colonel Yakov. Peter never saw the pathetic creature again. A more ruthless and less talkative team of interrogators replaced him. For over a week Peter suffered much the same treatment as he had endured at Dominica. Deprived of sleep by the searing arc lights in his cell, never alone for a moment, he was subjected to continuous questioning, day and night, until his mind reeled from the strain. Two interrogators took Cronin's place, and they relieved each other alternately, so that not for a single moment in these nightmare days and nights did Peter have a chance to relax his mind.

"Name, rank, number; that's all. Name, rank, number…" he mumbled brokenly after the end of the first week. He'd muttered nothing else since the brainwashing first started, he didn't know now how long ago. There was only one object in life, and that was to resist, to hold out against these human devils. Time was on his side, he kept repeating to himself, time's on our side … and he took comfort in knowing that every day he held out was one day nearer Commonwealth Day. They weren't going to incriminate the Bishop through him… Name, rank, number, name, rank…

Through the blue haze of tobacco smoke he gradually noticed that the devil who had been sitting in front of him had stood up. He was changing his tone now. No longer silky, he rapped the desk angrily, snapping the crazy thread that was running through Peter's mind.

"You're going to the Colonel now."

Peter felt the sudden fresh air when they frogmarched him down the flagged corridor. They came to a massive soundproofed door, over the lintel a notice: "Head of the Security Organisation, Free West Indies."

The door swung open.

Sitting behind the desk there lolled the dapper figure of Colonel Yakov, immaculately turned out. He was dressed in khaki drill, but he wore no insignia of rank or decorations. The tunic buttoned to the neck, eastern fashion, and this made him sweat. He looked at Peter as he entered, the expressionless eyes boring into him, piercing him to his very soul. The Tartar eyes were a hard, light-blue, searching and merciless. The high cheekbones betrayed his origin, while the way in which he had smoothed down his hair, black and shiny from the scented spirits of lime water, betrayed a military upbringing — might almost have been a Guards officer, Peter thought, now thoroughly alert. The fresh air had brought his reeling mind back to sanity, and now his brain was sending out danger signals: *this man was dangerous, beware of the deceptive calm, watch out, you've an adversary here…*

"Sinclair, I believe?" the man Yakov purred. "You're proving an obstinate fellow, you know. We have a saying in my country, 'It is the wise farmer who cuts his losses,' but you do not think so, eh?"

Peter remained silent. He wanted to know what had happened to Bill.

"You make only trouble for yourself. What is worse, I think, is that you are causing your friend Hawkins much pain. He is receiving treatment at this moment. A word from you could stop it…"

Peter suddenly laid about him, hurling the guards backwards. He leapt at Yakov, but they grabbed him, savagely twisting his arms behind his back. He cried out with pain.

"Not so fast, my friend, we have plenty of time."

Colonel Yakov watched his struggling prisoner with amusement.

"May I enlighten you a little? You presume too much you know. The trouble with you British is that you never know when you're licked." The suavity of his voice changed to anger. "M-make him stand up, guard!"

Peter felt a blow in the base of his spine and he quivered with the sudden pain. He was forced to stand upright. He faced Yakov with contempt.

"You make me sick, Yakov," Peter gasped. "Your system stands condemned by its contempt for human life and dignity. Mental and physical torture is part of your establishment, as the Houses of Parliament are part of ours." The Briton, deathly white of face, stared at the representative of Communism without flinching. "Keep your dirty system. I prefer my freedom, imperfect though it is."

Yakov said nothing. He rose from his chair and sat upon the corner of the desk nearest to Peter. With one leg stretched before him, he swung the other while he manicured his nails with the end of a dagger-shaped paperknife. He did not look up and his voice was only just audible when he spoke. He hissed his syllables and Peter felt the back of his neck prickling. The Colonel reminded him too much of the reptiles Peter had heard rustling in the black crate on Castries Square.

"So the Englishman speaks, eh? Has he finished his little s-speech?" Yakov turned towards his captive. He looked up, and though he met Peter's eyes momentarily, he could not hold his gaze. He was smiling, and the smooth face wore a mask of reasonableness. Then Peter received a shock.

Though Yakov smiled, Peter had rarely seen such an ice-cold, ruthless and impersonal mask. It was horrible meeting those reptilian eyes, even momentarily, and Peter shivered. In this sweltering heat he suddenly felt cold. He had a strange feeling that he'd met someone like this before, but though he wrenched at his confused brain he could not recall the memory. Yakov had turned away. He was talking aloud and staring out of the deep casement.

"It's such a pity, you know, Sinclair." Now he was all reasonableness and rational persuasion. "You and I could get along famously. You're bound to succumb in the end, you know. You see, I hold all the cards. There's nothing for you to live for: your friend's been shot, your submarine sunk."

Peter did not hear him at first, his mind far away. Yakov turned around and saw that his words were wasted: the fool was almost unconscious...

Yakov repeated his statement more loudly, and Peter grasped the words from somewhere far away. Their significance slowly drifted into his mind and then he felt a stinging pain across his left cheek.

"Wake up, will you, when I'm talking? I see I'll have to teach you manners."

Peter saw the soulless eyes less than a yard from him. Though Yakov's face twitched for self-control, the eyes betrayed nothing, not even rage. It was like facing a cobra — horrible and spine-chilling.

Peter laughed in the devil's face. He'd won Round One and his enemy knew it. It wasn't often that Yakov betrayed emotion in front of his captives, and then he suddenly realised that there was something unusual about this prisoner: he'd have to go more carefully. He turned away; he'd soon bring the Briton to heel. But Peter noticed Yakov's hands trembling with the effort of controlling his rage, and when he spoke he could not prevent the slight impairment in his speech.

"T-t-take care, S-sinclair," he stuttered, and he slurred the next words in his anger, "ye shouldn'a fash me". He turned away quickly from his adversary, his neck stiff and pugnacious as he peered hurriedly out of the window. In the surge of sudden rage he'd made a fatal slip, and the missing link now clicked in Peter's brain.

It's impossible, Peter thought, *quite out of the question. I couldn'a have heard aright,* and he used the quaint words himself. Totalitarian policemen don't use Scottish phrases; his mind must be playing him tricks. The swine must be breaking him down, the brainwashing machine was churning to its horrible, inevitable end. The human mind was like a medicine bottle; it could only hold so much courage and once the bottom was reached there was nothing left, no more to draw upon. Hadn't that been discovered in Hitler's war and in Korea? And he groaned when he thought of *Rugged*, twisted and torn, a broken thing, on the bottom of Tortola Bay. This devil may not be telling the truth, probably wasn't, and was only using this to break down his resistance. But why had he been fool enough to use a Scottish idiom? Why couldn't Peter break away from the feeling that he'd known someone like this before? And then Yakov swung round, his body under complete control.

The two men faced each other, implacable enemies, diametrically opposed, unconsciously representing the struggle that split the world. Then Peter was certain. The hard soulless eyes betrayed the identity. But Peter still could not credit it, the odds were too long ... and he racked his brain to clinch his suspicions.

He laughed insolently in Yakov's face. "You useless liar, Yakov. D'you expect me to believe that?" Peter continued, goading his tormentor. "You're a bigger oaf than I took you for!"

As Peter watched, he saw the colour mounting in Yakov's face. He saw the evil eyes watching him, cold and calculating, devoid of hate or emotion, and then Peter knew where he'd seen such amazing eyes before... Bermuda, Hillyard, Tom Hillyard... Even the stutter was there. Impossible, but true...

"Tom Hillyard!" Peter shouted, as Yakov's arm arched to strike.

Peter saw the eyes gazing at him from far away, blue and ice-cold... The room spun round him and he knew no more.

From far away, miles away, aeons away, a pinpoint of light was streaming. He fixed his eyes upon it while his mind slowly registered the criss-cross pattern that chequered the brightness. He tried to move towards it, but couldn't. He struggled, but felt a lifeless weight upon him, a deadweight that was pinning him down. He smelt the mustiness of dirty straw and then he regained consciousness. A moment of panic swept over him and he felt his heart racing as he shoved at the dead weight that was smothering him. The thing slithered off his chest and he grappled with it with his hands.

"Bill! Bill Hawkins!"

Peter scrambled to his knees; he dragged the senseless body through the straw until Bill's back slumped against one of the slimy pillars which supported the roof. Then Peter left him to search for water. His knees felt groggy but he could just stand upright in the filthy cell.

It was a large dungeon. Thick pillars supported the roof at intervals, and at the far end was a small casement window. Peter kicked at the straw as he approached the only source of air, but there was no hope of escape there. The wall was a good six feet thick, and the casement narrowed at the far end to less than a foot in height and only a few inches in width.

He felt the walls. They were wet and slimy with years of neglect, and in the corner he heard the pattering of rats. He stood still, and above the pounding of his heart he could hear the faint squealing of the vermin as they foraged in the straw. He shivered and felt the skin prickling at the back of his neck. He moved carefully towards them and approached the door gingerly. The rats were so bold that one scampered over his foot as it gambolled with a scrap of rotten fruit. Peter shuddered and pulled himself together. If rats were to be their companions, they might as well make the best of them. And he started pounding with his fists upon the massive door.

To his surprise there was an immediate rattling of keys in the lock and then, as Peter stood back, the door swung open to admit a solemn jailer. By his appearance, he was obviously the senior of the three soldiers who sniggered outside. The jailer shouted at his subordinates and then he entered, closing the door behind him.

"What d'you want?" he demanded.

"Water. My friend is hurt."

The guard was a ponderous man, but swift in his movements. He strolled over to Bill and shook him. He slapped his face, but, strangely, there was no viciousness in the blows.

"Keep silent. I get water."

To Peter's surprise, the man returned a few minutes later with a small bottle of water. Shutting the door carefully behind him, he went to Hawkins and gently dribbled a few drops through the cracked lips. Then he splashed the exhausted face. Peter watched in amazement. In a few minutes Bill Hawkins was shaking his lion-like head, and then the blue eyes rolled in their sockets until they focused upon the speck of light at the far end of the dungeon. The black guard stood the while over him, watching him, and Peter thought he almost detected a look of compassion upon the man's face.

"Why do you do this?" Peter asked. Hawkins was conscious and rubbing the back of his head.

"I also was a Christian, sah." The man turned to Peter. His face was sad and the eyes that looked at him were round and large, like a spaniel's. But then a shadow of fear crossed his face and he looked round quickly towards the door.

"I must go. I have been too long already." He shuffled quickly through the straw. "I am on guard, but I will be back."

The door swung ponderously, and in the sudden silence Peter stood bewildered. He mussed his tousled head and returned to Bill, who was moaning with the excruciating pain in his head.

"Cheer up, Bill! Come on, old chap, at least we're alive. Did they give you hell?"

The seaman nodded slowly. He'd had a hard time... He lifted his hand and pointed to his shoulders. Peter pushed back the shirt and gasped when he saw the weals.

"Poor old chap..." He paused before asking the next question. "Did you hold on?"

"Yes, sir. The devils got nothing from me. I think I passed out..."

Peter held the bottle to Bill's lips, and the sailor relaxed as he felt the liquid trickling down his throat. His eyes lit up as he gratefully acknowledged the gentleness of his companion. There was suddenly a flash of mutual respect between these two men, a feeling that nothing in this world could harm or sever their comradeship. Neither said much but each knew what the other felt. It was a tie, a bond of affection that nothing but death could end; of a quality that few men experienced, and then only in the heat of battle. It was something no civilian could understand and it was the turning point in their will to resist. They knew now that neither had succumbed; they had both withstood the devilish worst of their enemies, even until merciful oblivion released them, and they took comfort in this. They talked for a while, each taking courage from the other. The nightmare was beginning and there seemed no end to the long, black tunnel.

"What's happened to Hank, do you think, sir? The swine told me they'd caught and shot him."

"You can't ever believe a Commie, Bill. Truth isn't part of their make-up. It depends what suits them at the time: if lies will help, they lie; they tell the truth only if it's to their advantage."

"Yes, I know, sir. The whole world knows that, even themselves. But they might be right about Hank, sir. I mean Lootenant Jefferson, sir."

"He hadn't much of a chance, I admit. But you know Hank — remember Dubrovnik, Bill? It seems a long time ago now, doesn't it?"

Peter did not believe his own optimism. He was sick inside. Hank hadn't a chance.

"Bloomin' ages, sir. 'Ullo, what's this?" Bill half rose from the straw as the door opened. The sergeant of the guard entered, shutting the door swiftly behind him.

"You must be ready to see the Colonel, sah. Officer coming for you in half an hour. You must be ready."

"What time is it? They've taken our watches."

"Eight-thirty, masters; it will soon be night. For you, torture tonight they are preparing." Suddenly the words poured from the man's lips. "I come because I do not like these things. Once I was a Christian… I loved the Bishop. He good man. I no like it … no like it, masters." The wretched man shook his head, misery in his face.

"Why d'you take part in these things then?" Peter asked roughly. He had little time for whining, but it was different when it came from the man who was on top.

Before the guard would continue, he walked round the dungeon, checking the crevices for microphones. Apparently they hadn't got round to wiring them up yet, but he took much care over the rectangular hatchway in the centre of the ceiling. It had an iron frame and was hinged along one side. *Probably the old coal chute*, Peter thought, *when this was a country club.* But it was a massive thing, too high to reach from the floor, and protected by some sort of netting. There was little hope of escape that way, but the guard was satisfied that it concealed no microphone, and he returned to the waiting prisoners.

"*They* hold hostage my mother … my old mother, and my sister. If I do not work for the Communists they deal with my family. You know what that means…" and the man's voice trailed off brokenly. "I don't know what to do, masters."

Peter was silent a moment, and he looked across at Bill. Here was a ray of hope.

"Will you help us?"

The guard shook his head and his great round face was gleaming with sweat. He was struggling with himself, but the fear of reprisals upon his family was too strong. He could not help actively.

"Tell us," Peter commanded. "When are they sacrificing the Bishop, and where?"

"Don't you know?" The whites of the eyes rolled with unbelief in the ebony face. "The Day of Rebellion is on Commonwealth Day. The King will be in Trinidad and the Freedom Rally is to be on the Asphalt Lake."

"How do you know?" Bill snapped suspiciously, his eyes slits in his bruised face. He personally didn't like this man and perhaps he was a 'plant'? They had been tricked once. The whole business was one big lie, and even now he and the Captain weren't certain whether *Rugged* was lying sunk on the bottom of Tortola Bay, whether Hank was dead or alive…

"I have been detailed, masters, as one of the party to go to Trinidad. The steamer comes in two days and four platoons are going. I don't like it because many of us are still fond of the Bishop. He a good man, a verra good man, sah." The simple soul was near to tears. He was pouring out his soul now, like a flood bursting the lock gates. For over a year he'd been blackmailed into serving his Communist overlords, and there was no way out; but at least he could talk now to two other Christians. They understood and forgave…

"The Bishop great man, masters. He fought these bad things and many follow him, many, many…" He held his arms out wide in a sweeping gesture. "Not all West Indians bad, masters. But we have to do as we are told. No food otherwise; families starve." The broken sentences tumbled from the wretched man's lips.

"But surely, what about the U.N.I.C.E.F.?" Peter asked. "Thousands of tons of food have been delivered."

"To the ports, yes, masters. But the traitor merchants confiscate the food, and sell to the highest bidder. The poor no see the food, masters, and if we complain *they* stop supplies. It's no good, masters, my family starve if I no work for these people." He lifted his eyes to the roof. "The Colonel, he shoot me if he hear me speaking to you — but I can't help it, me no good..." The tears welled into the bloodshot eyes.

The lock rattled and the jailer jumped as if he'd been electrocuted. He looked apprehensively at Peter and Bill and then Bill dropped back into the straw. Peter slid to the other side of the pillar and from there he could hear Bill moaning softly. The door swung creakily on its hinges.

"You're a long time, Sergeant Cheetham. The Colonel wants to see the prisoners."

"Now, sah?"

"Yes, and hurry up about it. We want to get it over before dark."

"The swine are barely conscious, sah. Dere's little point in giving them 'the treatment'. I've just tried a little myself, sah." The guard sniggered. "It's a waste of time. They don't feel much in their condition."

"He wants a last interrogation before..." The dapper officer in the peaked cap grinned as he lifted his eyes to the trap in the centre of the ceiling.

Bill protested when he was lugged to his feet, and Peter had to help him to stand. In their hearts they were both dreading this second ordeal because they knew now that a decision had already been taken, should they hold out. But Peter felt no fear now: *Rugged* and all her gallant crew were sunk and lying in twenty fathoms of water; Hank lay dead and in less than a week the Rebellion would have started with the execution of the Bishop. He groaned in his agony of spirit. They reached the courtyard as the sun plummeted below the horizon.

The shadows criss-crossed the dirt of the square; the walls and the old fountain in the centre glowed pink and soft in the last rays of the sunset. They started to cross the courtyard and Peter was interested to see, in the middle by the fountain, the black crate and the casket they'd noticed at the rally in Castries. Two sentries lolled against the ancient parapet and they were smoking. The crate stood in the centre of the circular fountain, and the casket, a mahogany affair, was resting on top. As they marched by, Peter thought he could hear the hissing and rustling of the fer-de-lance in the crate, and he shivered. The sentries took little notice of the officer, but they grinned when they saw the two victims. They whispered together and Peter heard them chuckling. Evidently Bill and he were to be the centre of entertainment, and Peter felt a nightmarish quality of unreality sweeping over him. They'd endured so much already, surely there couldn't be much more?

His head started swimming as they passed through the arched gateway. They marched along the tarmac of the road which led to the Direktor's house, a modern villa two hundred yards from the archway. Judging by the mounds of rubble in the surrounds, the house could not have been finished long.

Peter was amazed to see how little the Country Club had changed since he'd played tennis here as a midshipman. The Direktor's house took up most of the old courts, but otherwise there was little difference. The low-lying spur swept down to the bay, and the mosquitoes were about already; he could hear their whine and wanted to swat them but couldn't because of his bonds. The enemy hadn't completed the perimeter fence yet, and like everything in this part of the world, it would be ages before it was finished. But the Direktor's house was wire-fenced and a red notice warned off intruders: it was alive with high-voltage. Things were different in the Direktor's domain. Efficiency reigned here at least, and Peter could see two sentries patrolling the grounds, one with a tracker dog.

At the rear of the house was a single-storeyed, flat-roofed building of some size. The walls were massively thick, and from one end a tall chimney protruded. Peter was astonished at the detail expended on this building; it had been well designed, he could see that. It would fulfil efficiently its function as a modern torture chamber, and he felt nauseated when he saw the extractor fans spinning in the opaque glass of the windows. Large, open drains ran from one room at the far end, and he saw Bill blanch as they walked to the back entrance.

In the last few yards of their journey Peter suddenly realised that they were glimpsing this world for the last time. As soon as Yakov realised there would be no capitulation, or if the confession was not in time for the Bishop's execution next week, the Colonel would liquidate them. How, mattered little, yet Peter shivered. And the devilish cleverness of Yakov, alias Tom Hillyard, suddenly struck the young Englishman. What effrontery, and how the traitor had fooled them all in Bermuda! Peter felt hot when he remembered their friendship.

They stood before the Colonel in the interrogating room, and as Peter looked at the mobile face smiling sardonically at him, he realised the brilliance of this spy. An expert at disguise, he had a fluid face, without any distinctive feature, the look of a very ordinary man, one that you could not pick out in a crowd. Admittedly the cheekbones were slightly higher than an Englishman's, but with the military moustache that he'd worn as Tom Hillyard, that distinction went unnoticed. No, his only characteristics were his stutter when incensed and the peculiar light blue and expressionless quality of his eyes. He was watching disinterestedly as Peter entered, as a snake mesmerises its prey.

Peter spoke first. "You swine, Hillyard! You'd cut your grandmother's throat, if it suited you!"

Yakov did not move. Peter heard the ticking of the clock on his desk.

"Perhaps … it depends if so doing would serve the Party." Then Yakov sidled towards Peter. "But you must admit I was good as Tom Hillyard. The sad thing is that you have recognised me. Unfortunate for you, that is."

Peter could play perhaps for time. It depended upon when Bill would lose his temper. Peter could see him beginning to boil already.

Yakov continued: "I won't be able to return to Bermuda anyway, it's too risky now. I'll have to get '*my son*' out. Pity! He's enjoying working with the Wrens at The Princess. He'll miss 'em — they were much better at deciphering than he was."

Flippancy always irritated Peter and now he wanted to shove Yakov's tongue back down its gullet.

"What are you going to do with us, Yakov?"

The Direktor pulled at his Russian-type cigarette, a long, thin tube of sweet-smelling tobacco. He was in no hurry and the contest amused him. He flicked the ash on to the carpet.

"I'm going to try and make you sign a confession, Sinclair. But if you and your friend refuse, you're both going to end up somewhat unpleasantly." The corners of his mouth curled as he gazed upon this Englishman. "The choice is yours. It's up to you… You see, there's really no point in continuing your stay with us if you refuse. You'd be a liability because you have recognised Tom Hillyard. If you escape, you will disclose our whole information net. If you remain here as our — er... guests, you will require feeding, and that is rather wasteful these days... No, I've had enough of you. Sign the documents, please, or take the consequences."

"Show me," Peter said quietly. "I don't sign anything without reading it first."

Yakov struck Peter hard across the face, and it hurt. The blow landed where he'd been hit before and he felt blood oozing from the corner of his mouth.

"The confession merely incriminates the Bishop of the Antilles and yourselves as agents, that's all."

Peter spoke softly: "And once we've signed, you'll kill us anyway. I'm having nothing to do with it."

"And what about your sailor friend? Hawkins, isn't he?"

Bill's reply was unprintable. Yakov flushed, then nodded at the guards. Cheetham took charge of the escort and they were frogmarched from the room, Yakov accompanying them back to the courtyard of the barracks. He halted the party in the centre of the square.

"Throw back the cover!"

The Direktor whispered the order. He was enjoying this.

Cheetham approached the crate gingerly. He flipped the black protecting cloth backwards. In front of him was a sheet of thick plate glass, one side of the reptile crate. Peter gasped.

"Not very pleasant, are they?" Yakov asked quietly. "I'm sure you have noticed that this crate has a hinged floor, Sinclair?"

The fountain stood over the heavy hatch that was built into the ceiling of their dungeon.

"Ah, so you begin to see, Sinclair? Rather neat, eh...?"

Yakov went up to the plate glass. He tapped the side with his finger. Suddenly the whole floor of the box started to undulate. Black coils twisted and a mass of spitting serpents writhed upwards. Their reptilian eyes gazed directly at their tormentors, and the forked tongues flickered angrily. Their jaws opened wide and the wicked fangs of the fer-de-lance showed yellow and foul. Peter wanted to be sick. He looked away.

From somewhere far away he heard the oily voice of the Direktor.

"If you remember your school physics, you will remember your facts on expansion. There is rather a cunning little device on this cage. When this courtyard reaches its midday temperature, the catch on the floor of the cage expands. This completes an electrical circuit, and the floor of the crate is drawn back by a servomotor. As the cage is directly over your cell, we'll remove the hatch in the ceiling and then, when the cage floor is withdrawn at midday tomorrow, these interesting reptiles will drop down on you for company. We'll be watching from above, so you won't be lonely. It ought to be interesting, but I'm afraid the experiment won't be very useful."

"Why, you devil? Why d'you do this?" Peter whispered, barely able to speak.

"Because I hope you will sign. I'm sure you will, Sinclair … there's not much to live for now, is there?" Yakov smiled with his face. But his eyes were cold like those of his snakes.

Yakov snapped his fingers and the guards replaced the covering.

"Don't want to spoil their appetites, you know," Yakov grinned. "They haven't very long to wait before their daily meal. Goodnight, gentlemen. If you change your minds, tell the guards. Remember, I hate being disturbed at night."

The darkness of a tropical night had already fallen as Yakov's retreating figure reached the gateway.

CHAPTER 11

Serpent Executioners

It wasn't the mustiness of the straw and the playfulness of the rats that kept Peter and Bill awake.

In the middle of the ceiling there was now a thick glass plate. This floor of the reptile cage was transparent because it was illuminated from above by powerful arc lamps which both irritated and kept awake the snakes.

Peter approached only once the middle of the room to inspect their executioners. The writhing mass of fer-de-lance made him nauseated and he looked away. He would never forget the evil, the dispassionate, the calculating eyes that glinted expectantly above him. Their forked tongues flickered, their jaws opening to display the incurving fangs, and their flat heads waved upon their erect necks. They were a loathsome and terrifying sight.

"Don't like 'em, sir. Nasty, I'd call 'em, yes, definitely nasty."

Hawkins gently took his Captain by the arm and led him back to their corner by the pillar. Even the rats congregated there, away from the central cage: they also had seen the snakes.

"Let's try to sleep, sir. There ain't much we can do before the morning. Don't feel like disturbing the Colonel myself."

Bill forced Peter down into the straw and they both turned on their sides in an attempt at sleep. But it must have been well after midnight that Peter finally lost consciousness, and then he dozed only fitfully. He remembered Cheetham coming to change the guards outside the door and then he had visited his prisoners. But he had kept silent and stayed away from the middle of the dungeon. He'd be back in the morning watch, he'd said, and he was going to get his head down. Peter had the germ of an idea in the recesses of his mind, but he wanted to sleep before tackling Cheetham. The unhappy man seemed their only hope of escape, but the two prisoners must refresh themselves first. They were exhausted.

It was in the early hours that Peter first heard the baying of hounds. He turned on his back and thought he was waking from the agonies of a nightmare, but by the time he'd regained consciousness the barking had stopped. He turned on his side again and tried to sleep. The light from the central glass panel in the ceiling was percolating dimly through the cell, but already it seemed less bright. The new day was breaking, their last day on earth, and he felt his stomach heave.

What a horrible death lay before them! Already he could visualize the sun climbing from the eastern horizon, gold and red in its majesty, burning with its elemental heat, the powerhouse of this planet; but also the unwitting executioner of two Englishmen when it reached its zenith. He shuddered and silently shook the lethargy from his mind. He climbed to his feet, and as the straw rustled Bill jerked awake. His eyes were shining, and he was poised on his feet, ready for anything. Only his face betrayed his recent ordeal. There was a purple bruise below the left cheekbone and his face was grey with strain and weariness. He passed a hand over his eyes and turned away from the arc lights.

"Bill, I'm not waiting here to be eaten by those things, are you?" Peter nodded towards the writhing coils above them.

"What'll we do, sir? I'd rather be shot down in cold blood than wrestle with them snakes. I'll do anything rather than have to face those things, sir, anything..." There was a note of hysteria in Bill's voice. Peter recognised the approach of collapse and he felt a sense of futility creeping over himself. He was mesmerised by the wicked eyes glinting from the cage above them, and he felt there was little that they could do now. But, as Bill said, better to be shot down in cold blood than have to face this hissing death…

"When Cheetham returns, Bill, I'll talk to him while you nobble him from behind. He's on duty for the morning…" and as he finished the sentence there was a rattling in the lock. The watch was being changed.

"Quick, Bill! Behind the door! It's now or never."

Bill slipped behind the door which was starting to swing. Then the hunched figure of the Sergeant of the Guard entered. He was carrying a torch and was followed by the tall figure of the Officer of the Guard. The door shut behind them. The Officer of the Guard had drawn his pistol: he was taking no chances. The Sergeant seemed nervous, his eyes darting between Peter and Bill. The officer kept his head averted and his peaked cap concealed his face in shadow. Peter dared not rush them now, they hadn't a chance with that drawn gun. Then the officer turned his face towards them.

"You goddarned Limeys! Can't you recognise me?"

The tall officer bounded towards Peter. Hank, the indestructible Yank! Peter could hear Bill choking in the corner. "My God, oh, my God!" he was whispering, "my God…" and the seaman stumbled towards the American with his arms outstretched.

"Hold on, old fellow," Hank said. "We'll soon be out of here. This wonderful guy," he said, as he clapped his arm round the silent Cheetham, "this guy got me in and he's got to get us out. Come on, hitch up your belts, lads! We're getting out now, before dawn's too well on. Get going, Cheetham."

The black guard opened the door gingerly. He peered through the crack in the door and then they stepped over two crumpled bodies that lay on the flagstones outside. Cheetham led the way up the spiralling staircase until they reached the fresh air of the courtyard. Already day was breaking, the first light showing in silver streaks behind the silhouette of the roofs. Three more bodies were dead in the dust. One lay by the gateway while two others sprawled near the disused fountain in the centre of the yard. The casket of the Sacred Belt lay on top of the serpents' crate, and its bands shone in the first rays of the sun.

"Let's grab it, Hank!" Peter whispered, and he started to move towards it.

But Hank reached it first and he grunted when he tried to lift the casket.

"Too heavy," he whispered. "We've got a lot of running to do, chum."

But Peter hesitated a moment, the germs of an idea in his mind. He noticed a heap of builder's sand lying in a corner of the yard.

While Hank trussed up the co-operative Sergeant of the Guard with an odd length of telegraph wire that was littering the yard, Peter and Bill lugged the casket over to the sand heap. They lowered the massive wooden box to the ground and then they heard Hank come loping towards them. "The guard's given me the key. For Pete's sake get a hustle on! Our luck can't hold much longer," he whispered. Peter heard him cocking his revolver. Then Hank retreated to the gateway where he could cover them all.

With a little persuasion from Bill, the lid sprung open. Peter snatched the glittering Belt from the casket and snapped the ornament round his waist. Then they both shovelled with their hands like maniacs until the casket was full of the moist sand. Bill snapped the lid, tried it, found it had jammed shut, and then they both struggled with it back to the fountain. They dropped the casket back on top of the reptile cage and took a last look at the snakes spitting behind their glass wall. Peter bent over Cheetham. His face was serene behind the gag and the eyes were smiling. He'd done his duty to his conscience: at least he'd shown the Englishmen that the Bishop still retained some of his faithful; not all West Indians had sold their soul. Cheetham was happy at last, and he grunted farewell as Peter pressed his shoulder. From the corner of his eyes, Cheetham watched the escaping prisoners make their getaway. He saw them slipping through the gateway, past the dead man, and out on to the road. He heard the barking of a dog and then all was quiet once more. The guard shut his eyes and he was happy within himself for the first time in two years. He prayed the prisoners would get clear away…

As soon as Hank had passed the tennis courts, he broke into a loping trot. Encouraging and coaxing, he spurred his exhausted friends to one final spurt. He led them through the palm plantations, silent and deserted at this hour. It was still twilight when, panting for breath, they reached the turf slope leading to the beach on the western side of the spit. The palm leaves rustled above them and suddenly Peter felt soft sand beneath his feet. He sniffed the air and there, less than thirty yards away, he saw the surf breaking. How grand it was to feel the sea breeze and his heart filled with hope.

"Stay here and wait for my whistle," Hank whispered. "The helipad is behind that belt of palms, and I'm going to fix the sentry. Luckily, the natives seem as slap-happy with the Commies as they were with us. Ten to one the sentry's asleep."

Into the gloom Hank slipped, loosening his commando knife as he went.

"What's up, sir?" Bill asked in a whisper. "Can he fly those things?"

Peter was lying flat on his stomach and he felt his heart thumping against his ribs while they waited. How he longed to help, but he supposed the American knew what he was doing. Hank only had to bungle this and they would all face the firing squad … yes, it was now or never, and presumably Hank *could* pilot a helicopter or he wouldn't be trying this. Then above the murmur of the surf a faint whistle floated downwind.

They scrambled to their feet, and then they were running, running as fast as their aching legs would carry them. They were dimly aware of the boles of the palms rushing by, then, gasping and choking, they broke through the screen of trees. A rectangular pad of concrete edged the beach, and upon this was silhouetted the outlines of two helicopters against the western sky. Sikorskys, Peter judged. In the darkness by the control hut, Peter glimpsed two figures: the tall one stood over the other, a pistol in his hand. Peter rushed over and Hank took charge.

"We're in luck, Pete, this guy's the only one here till dawn. Take him, Pete. Make him help us on our take-off. This ought to persuade him." He handed the gun to Peter.

Hank ran on ahead and leapt into the helicopter while Peter and Bill forced the protesting guard on to the concrete. Peter saw the lights in the cockpit and then, as he neared the plane, Hank's face appeared at the door. He was grinning from ear to ear.

"Piece of cake, Pete! This is a Sikorsky and I can fly it blindfold! I had a squadron of them when I was at Kinley. Come on, Bill. Start her up, Pete."

The guard had no intention of laying down his life for the cause of Communism. The engine whined, then clattered into life. While Hank checked the controls, Peter locked the sentry in the hut. A moment later the helicopter fluttered, then waltzed from the pad with the three friends on board.

Peter was watching through the port door as the ground floated away beneath them. As they crossed the line of surf, Peter saw men running through the palms. They knelt down suddenly and raised guns to their shoulders. A line of jagged holes pierced the fuselage behind Bill's head, but there was no sound.

The plane flew on unscathed and Peter yelled in Hank's ear: "Fly north until we're out of sight. I'll give you a course in a minute."

Hank nodded and the tail lurched round. Suddenly the sun climbed from the eastern horizon and the spinning tail rotor gleamed in its rays. St. Lucia was already taking on the shape of an island and fast disappearing on their starboard quarter. They must throw off their pursuers before their fighters became airborne.

"Course three-five-o for twelve minutes, Hank," Peter shouted. "Then bring her round to south. We'll go out to sea for a bit. They shouldn't look for us out here."

Hank nodded, then tapped the fuel indicator. It was only half full. He leant downwards and yelled at Peter:

"Less than a hundred and fifty miles flying, at eighty knots, Pete. Where will that bring us?"

Peter pricked off the arc along the latitude scale.

"Steer one-nine-five, Hank, that'll keep us out to sea. We ought to sight Grenada in an hour and a half."

"If the fuel lasts out," Hank shouted back as he tapped the gauge. The pointer had already dropped down the scale...

But their hopes stood higher now. They'd got as far as this and why shouldn't they try to reach Trinidad in time for the Freedom Rally? They might even be able to put a spoke in their enemies' plans. In their present state of mind they were obsessed with the power of the Serpent King and his hold over the terrified population. They reminded themselves that this nightmare world was not the natural order of things, but merely an imposed tyranny that could be rejected. The battle took place in men's minds. Then they knew that at all costs they must reach Trinidad and try to rescue the Bishop before it was too late.

Peter chuckled as he felt the weight of the Sacred Belt about him. He lifted his shirt from his trousers and slipped the gold Belt from his waist. The object thumped to the floor of the plane and its rubies glowed from their golden settings. It was an ancient ornament, but the craftsmen had not finished the job properly. The glowing rubies were set skilfully in the golden coils and head of the fer-de-lance, but the articulation was weak, the hinges merely held together by rusting nails.

With a feeling of revulsion he showed the ornament to Bill. As Peter started wrapping it round his waist again, he thought he heard a shout from Bill, but he did not look up. The rotors were threshing loudly above them (Hank had the doors open in the growing warmth of the morning) and their flutter was making conversation impossible. Then Peter felt a dig in the back. He turned round. Bill leant with one hand against the frame of the open door. Through the opening Peter could just make out the hazy outline of St. Lucia. Low cloud was sweeping out towards them, and already the blueness of the sea was disappearing to the eastwards. There was a clammy coldness about them, and Peter instinctively knew that fog was about. But Bill was shouting excitedly, and with his other hand he was pointing towards a speck that grew larger at every second.

"Aircraft, sir, port quarter!" he yelled. "It's a fighter and she's gaining fast!"

CHAPTER 12

The Piffle-Wurfer

"Clear the bridge! Dive, dive, dive!"

The water was already halfway up the fin when the launching arty scrambled down the hatch. Benson jumped down on some unfortunate's head, and then the first clip was on.

"Eighty feet, Pilot!" he yelled from the darkness. "Full ahead. Shut off from depth-charge attack!"

These nuclears were slow, infernally slow in diving. Admittedly *Rugged* was a Mark II, but nevertheless, she took a minute longer to get under than her Mediterranean forebear. Sixty seconds can seem an eternity when four thousand tons of destroyer are hurtling towards you at thirty knots, at less than a thousand yards.

"Switch to white lighting."

The gloom of the red lamps was depressing and Benson felt better when the lighting returned to normal. He seemed to have a crisis on his hands though he'd been in command less than five minutes.

"Five hundred yards, sir."

Elliott looked up from his set and smiled at his new Captain. What a raw deal! The chap hadn't a chance when Goddard sighted the destroyers: Sinclair was already on his way shorewards and could have done nothing. Now Benson needed all the support and confidence they could give him. He was their Captain for the moment and upon his decisions their fate depended.

"Sixty feet, sir. Permission to pump?" Taggart asked as the last roarings of 'Q' vented inboard. But then the thunder of the attacking destroyer swamped everything — a Royal Marine band beating the retreat in the fore-ends would not have mattered at this moment. The hunter was running down *Rugged*'s slick and would unload her patterns on the submarine's diving swirl…

Click — click —

Benson sickened when he heard the strikers spring home in the primers … the depth charges must be tumbling down through the water at this moment … and he wondered abstractedly what the modern depth charge would be like.

"Eighty feet, sir. Boat shut off from depth-charge attack."

"Very good. Steer one-nine-o."

"Steer one-nine-o, sir," Able Seaman Bowles reported calmly. The men were good to him. There could have been few men of his age who'd held a nuclear command for less than ten minutes and yet had been depth-charged within that time. No one knew the lethal range of a nuclear depth charge yet…

Benson steadied himself at the ladder. He saw Elliott removing his headset, and as the H.S.D. turned towards him their restricted world stood still for a split second. No one really heard the explosion; the shock was physical, and seemed soundless.

"Nuclear…?" Benson gasped. The charges were countermining each other and exploding in ripples around them. *More like mortars hitting the bottom*, he thought. *If one lands on us…*

The boat jumped at each shock and Benson recoiled from the ship's side with each hammer blow that made it spring inwards. The power of the explosions was elemental, shattering.

The lights jerked in their holders and went out. Momentarily there was darkness until the emergency lamps flickered on. In their pale light Benson saw the Coxswain crossing himself. *If that experienced man is worried*, the thought flashed through Benson's mind, *the heat must be pretty near* ... he glanced at the depth: ninety feet, and miraculously still under control, though dropping slowly. She'd bottom at twenty fathoms ... she couldn't withstand another hammering like this; if she stuck in the mud, their hunters could take their time and blast them to pieces. The rumble of the destroyer passed down their starboard side and Benson sighed. They were intact, at least.

"Destroyer in contact, sir. Transmission interval decreasing."

Benson swore softly. The hunters hadn't wasted much time up top; these boys were good. Already he could hear the tick-ticking of the Asdic impulses against the pressure hull — the maddening, insistent whisper permeated every sealed compartment and grated on men's nerves.

Tick-tick ... tick-tick...

"I'm getting out of this, Pilot. Can't see much point in sticking around here. Let's show them *Rugged*'s paces."

Taggart was wrestling with the trim and he nodded. He had his hands full. He was surprised to hear the next order.

"Stand by stern tubes! Full ahead on main motor, starboard five, steer two-five-o. I'm taking her out to sea, Pilot."

The Engine Room phone mewed and Thatcher snatched it from its socket. Was the reactor damaged? He turned anxiously towards the Captain.

"Engineer Officer, sir. Wants to speak to the Captain."

Benson's heart sank. "Chief? Yes, Captain speaking."

The Scot's voice seemed far away and in the rumble which increased with the power of her enormous screw, Benson found it difficult to hear.

"...lub oil tank. Slight leak started by last attack. Could be leaking to the surface through the valve-seating and leaving an oil slick. No, the pressure hull is O.K., the reactor undamaged. These new mountings, you know..."

"Thank you, Chief. Report if you manage to stop the leak."

Benson replaced the phone. If it was really so...

Then his mind clicked. Their only chance was to fool the enemy; he'd have to assume that there was no oil leak.

"Pilot, have we got those *piffle-wurfers* on board?"

Taggart laughed shortly. The boat was careering about from the full power and he was having trouble preventing her from waltzing about. He daren't touch bottom at this speed and depth: this was a rocky coast. Why the devil did Benson ask wet questions at this moment? Couldn't he see that Taggart had his hands full?

"*Piffle-wurfers*, sir? Those capsules the Germans used in the last war? They're in the locker under the chart table."

"Take half a dozen aft, Brock," Benson snapped. "After I've fired the stern tubes, drain down and reload with six *piffle-wurfers*. They may just give us the breathing space we need."

"Aye, aye, sir."

Brocklebank waited by the after bulkhead door while Thatcher took off the clips. The seaman was grinning. *The youngster didn't realise how close a neighbour Death was at this moment*, thought Brock, and then the seaman dived through the steel doorway.

"Tell the Division to watch out for torpedoes, Yeoman," the Group Commander shouted above the whining of the wind in the rigging. "A cornered rat's a dangerous swine; we must stamp on it, mustn't we, Captain?"

It was a starlit night, and as he looked astern he smiled at the splendid sight. On either quarter the ships of his Division were keeping perfect station in quarter line: an acknowledged tribute to the efficiency of his training over the past months. He'd always realised that some of his weaker captains had resented his ruthless methods, but now they could see for themselves that his singleness of purpose was paying off…

"Yes, sir. But this submarine's a crafty one. We're only just gaining on her. Thank goodness the helicopters can keep up…"

The two officers looked ahead at the hovering hunters. But they had to shield their faces from the slamming of the wind, and the Captain shied away to watch the boiling wake at his stern. What a splendid sight his ship made! He was very proud of her at this moment. He heard the Yeoman broadcasting on Manoeuvring Wave…

"From Group Captain to all ships. Beware…"

The Captain saw the Yeoman halt in his message and then he followed the man's outstretched arm as a low rumble echoed from the starboard quarter. The Captain jerked round. The Group Commander was too late. Ludvic, the new Commanding Officer in *El Presidente*, was a gonner, and the Captain felt sickened as he saw the bows of his friend's destroyer rearing into the air. A 'homing' torpedo probably. The ship hung for a moment, vertically poised, then she slipped suddenly downwards, a cauldron of steam and flame obscuring her as she slid beneath the surface.

"Port ten. All ships form line abreast!" the Commander shouted. This was war, the cruel war at sea which the Englishmen understood so well, and he rounded on the Captain of the destroyer that flew his flag. But before he could open his mouth the loudspeaker crackled.

"Ops — Bridge! Submarine contact, bearing right ahead, range two thousand yards. Target seems stationary, or else we're steaming right up her kilt!"

The Captain bounded to the Engine Room phone.

"Give her all you've got, Chief! We've got her this time!" he shouted down the mouthpiece. He spun round and yelled at the Officer of the Watch:

"Stand by a nuclear pattern!"

The tension in the Control Room was electric. The leading destroyer was streaking across her stern now, a flurry of water noises against the background H.E. of the rest of the squadron. If she picked up *Rugged* now, while the destroyer was doing thirty knots, there was little hope for the submarine which was slinking away silently at low speed, having doubled back on her tracks.

"Destroyer transmitting, sir, not in contact."

Benson sighed with relief. Perhaps he had deceived their hunter; perhaps the *piffle-wurfer* would hold the enemy's attention long enough for *Rugged* to make her getaway. Elliott could hear them transmitting on the Asdic decoy, but surely they wouldn't be fooled for long? Our destroyers soon distinguished them in the war, but then these people had not had the experience … as long as they were fooled at this moment was all that concerned *Rugged*.

The H.E. disappeared rapidly up their port side while Benson adjusted *Rugged*'s course to keep her stern-on. Men spoke in whispers and they wore gym-shoes to reduce all noise. Someone had only to drop a spanner now, and they were dead ducks.

"Can you give me a range?"

The H.S.D. readjusted his earphones and retuned his set.

"About five thousand yards, sir."

Benson crossed his fingers. Strange that no patterns had been dropped on the *piffle-wurfer* yet ... perhaps they were running clear of a nuclear pattern?

"Distance back to Tortola Bay, Brock?"

As Brocklebank stooped over the chart table a low rumble echoed and re-echoed against the pressure hull. They had heard nothing like this before, and then the shock wave hit them. The boat heaved momentarily, then took on a peculiar roll. She seemed to be picked up bodily and hurled forwards, tumbling almost end over end. They had to hold on to keep their balance and they saw the depth gauge pointers seesawing madly. Then gradually she settled down to her normal trim at two hundred feet.

"That gerfuffle ought to confuse them for a bit, Elliott. I reckon that was our first experience of a nuclear charge." Benson grinned. Mercifully they were well out of range.

"And I hope our last," Taggart chuckled.

But Elliott was standing up at his set, his hands to his ears. He had been caught with his headset on and the blast had nearly blown in his eardrums: the pain was excruciating. Benson moved hurriedly towards him.

"I'm all right, sir," Elliott said, and then he looked at his hands. They were smeared with blood.

"Take the H.S.D. for'd, please, Cox'n. Make him turn in and have him relieved, please, Pilot."

"Aye, aye, sir."

The Second Cox'n took over the after-planes and the Sub jumped to the fore-planes. There were murmurs of sympathy for Elliott as he staggered towards the bulkhead door. The clips were slipped off, the door swung open, and he was helped for'd to his Mess.

Rugged slunk away from her hunters and, when she came up from deep, there was nothing to be seen to the westward except an occasional star shell. She went deep again and continued to close Tortola Bay. They wouldn't look for her there, Benson reckoned, even if they thought she was still in the land of the living. He came to periscope depth at daybreak and made a perfect landfall: Tortola Bay right ahead. Taggart took over the periscope.

"Stand by for a fix, Brock… Left-hand edge, THAT…"

As the bearings were being read off from the bearing ring by the Stoker P.O., Taggart stiffened. He flicked to high-power and the speck magnified into a helicopter — might be a 'Sono' job…

"Captain, sir!"

Benson grabbed the periscope handles. Although the helicopter seemed to be climbing, she was flying straight towards them and was bound to spot them.

"Down periscope," he ordered. "Emergency change of depth — one hundred feet."

The klaxon roared, the doors swung shut, and *Rugged* was once more on her way down.

CHAPTER 13

The Evening Breeze

The Grande Anse was silent and still. It was midday and the heat of the sun was shimmering off the water. Fort St. George brooded silently over the natural harbour, long chains of bougainvillea trailing in purple festoons from its crumbling walls. This picturesque port of St. Georges, the capital of Grenada since time began, was a sleepy place even in the tunny season, so now, during the worst fishing season of the year, there was little to stir the fishermen from their lethargy. The oily calm was unruffled by even a breath of wind, and along the tumbledown wharf the schooners lay, their mainsails still hoisted. The brown canvas slatted idly, the peaks dropped for fear of sudden squalls.

In the shade that ran like a black finger along the edge of the sand bounding the Grande Anse lay three men. One was dressed in the light khaki drill of a Security Officer. He was tall and angular, while his companions, unshaven and unkempt, were of different builds. Short and stocky was the fair-haired one, the other wiry, well-built, but obviously a dissolute planter. They seemed to be taking their midday siesta, and no one bothered them. Only fools and Englishmen moved in this heat…

"Wish this was Blackpool, sir," Bill Hawkins murmured. "What wouldn't I give—"

"Dry up, Bill," Hank croaked. "I'm thirsty enough too. When I force-landed the kite I thought life was going to be easy. Didn't reckon we'd be dying of thirst."

"You're both lucky to be alive, so pack it up," Peter snapped irritably. "The helicopter started coughing as we touched down. We only just made it."

"D'you think anyone noticed us, sir? I mean, a 'copter ain't everyone's idea of routine, is it? But they won't learn much from her now."

"Yeah, that was sure a dandy idea of yours, Pete. She ought to be invisible in that depth of water. Better than setting fire to it, any day."

"I suppose some fisherman will foul his nets on it one day. At least *you* had a swim, Hank. You looked a bit undignified, though, as you crawled from the sea in your birthday suit."

"Better than getting these clothes wet, anyway. I've 'borrowed' the previous owner's 'akkers'. He must have been well paid by the Commies." Hank fished out a bundle of notes from a breast pocket.

And so they lay there until the evening, resting and planning their next moves. Hank recounted his escape in Castries; how he had planned the rescue and of the intended escape route: he'd had no trouble with the guards. They were chicken feed after his Mediterranean training ground. His luck had held when he'd stumbled upon the friendly guard, and after that it was easy. They'd been lucky too with the fog; the fighter soon lost them in the thick banks of white mist, and when they had emerged there had been no sign either of the aircraft or of St. Lucia.

"Come on," Peter said, when the shadows started to lengthen across the sand. "The port seems busier now and I'm hungry. Let's get cracking. We'll take the outer boat, because there'll be less disturbance slipping away from the wharf."

One at a time they climbed up to the roadway. They soon were lost in the bustling crowd which was enjoying itself in the cool of the evening amongst the market stalls.

Hank discovered that his uniform cleared a way through the jostling mass, and Peter and Bill stood back from the stalls whilst Hank bought fruit. The clamour was good to hear, and surely they would be safe here, away from the Secret Police that now honeycombed the islands.

Chickens clucked and flapped about their feet, children chased each other through the crowd, hurtling past their legs. The gaudy colours of the women contrasted with the more sober dress of the men, who wore cotton trousers and short-sleeved shirts. A group of fishermen were sitting on their haunches in one corner and they were humming the first lilting strains of a calypso. The instruments consisted of a petrol drum and a stretched wire along a wooden staff; but this was all they needed to strum the sad and plaintive refrain of their forefathers. The tempo thrummed and gained momentum. In no time a laughing, jostling crowd had gathered for the calypso. Suddenly the crowd became nervous, the singing trailed off, and then Peter saw the reason. Marching along the quayside swaggered three Secret Police; a sergeant and two troopers by the look of them. Peter nudged Bill, and they turned their backs on the inquisitive newcomers. They foraged amongst the fruit of a nearby stall while they watched Hank. In his uniform he was bound to be spotted. The singing trailed away to a silence that froze the crowd, and in that moment Peter knew they were discovered. This frieze of bewildered natives would be indelibly etched on his memory.

All eyes watched the tall officer by the fruit stall. Though the crowd had little time for politics, they sensed that the regime of their new masters brought fear and secrecy, and they liked it little. But anything was worth their final aspiration to freedom, and hadn't these new foreigners promised it? And wasn't this what they'd all been training and working for, during these two long years? They felt that the day of Liberation would be soon, very soon...

Peter held his breath. Hank was slowly turning over a grapefruit in his hand. He pressed it with his thumb and then slowly returned it to the stall. He shook his head, and then looked up, as if he'd just noticed the silence. He turned deliberately towards the three policemen. His eyes blazed angrily as he strode towards the sergeant.

"What the devil d'you mean by interrupting these people, Sergeant? Can't you see they're beginning their calypso?"

The astounded sergeant saluted rapidly, and Hank bundled the man out of earshot of the crowd.

"Where's your intelligence, man?" Hank blurted excitedly. "Haven't we told you, time and time again, not to annoy the natives?"

As Peter watched, he heard the crowd murmuring again; there was laughter and then, as they watched the officer administering the reprimand, they took up once more the refrain of their calypso. The oil drum thumped, the string whined, and in the rhythm of the music the incident was quickly forgotten.

"Phew!" Bill whispered in Peter's ear. "Thought we'd had our chips that time, sir."

"Come on. Follow me in a moment. Let's get down to the quay while the going's good. I've a horrible feeling that they're searching for us, Bill." Peter started to stroll after the officer, who was being given a respectful exit through the crowd.

The schooners were moored stern-first to the quay, and the level of the jetty was some ten feet lower than the roadway.

Peter sauntered down the stone steps, his hands in his pockets, a picture of slovenliness. Hank was talking to a grizzled old seaman, and then the American turned to glance with distaste at the unshaven planter who was slouching along the quay.

"Hullo, Brown! What d'you say to a night's fishing? The skipper says he'll take us if we want, but we'll have to pay dear for it. The tunny's not about yet, he says."

"Good evening, sir," Peter replied deferentially. "'Fraid I can't offer to pay, but me and my mate," he tossed his head towards Bill who was shambling down the jetty, "we'd be glad to lend you a hand, sir. It'd break the monotony of this dreary existence." Peter spat over the edge of the jetty.

The old fisherman watched the police officer, who seemed somewhat dubious as he considered his slatternly acquaintances. Then the officer shrugged his shoulders and started to search for his wallet.

"All right, Johnny. How much?" He flicked some notes between his fingers.

The old man's eyes glinted in the lined face. Hank and he settled the bargain, and then they clambered aboard the old schooner, the skipper going for'd to rouse his crew.

"Let them get us clear of the harbour," Peter whispered as they waited in the well by the wheel. "We'll nobble them when we get out of sight of land, or when darkness falls. Persuade him to take us northwards, Hank."

The old men watched with amusement from the quay when the schooner put to sea. Poor old Josiah, he'd never catch anything! He never did, at the best of times, and the onlookers shrugged their shoulders as the old *Moonstone* nudged her way out of the harbour. Her blocks squealed as she cleared the breakwater and then, as darkness stole rapidly upon them in the short twilight of the tropics, the onlookers saw her peak hove taut. She hovered for a moment while her headsails were set, the evening breeze filled her canvas, and she slowly vanished from sight.

"You want to fish, master?"

The skipper asked the question disgruntledly. He'd got the money now, and he didn't want to waste his crew's energy for nothing. Provided his visitors could be dissuaded from fishing, he would not have to share so much of the money with his idle crew.

Peter spoke up and addressed the police officer.

"We're quite happy just to enjoy the sail, sir. But of course, it's entirely up to you. You're paying for it, sir."

Hank reluctantly agreed.

"All right, Johnny. Give us a good sail, and we'll be happy. Go and turn in and leave the ship to us. She can come to no harm; there's little wind." He gazed upwards at the billowing sails that were just filling. "What course do you want us to steer?"

The old man seemed pleased at the suggestion, and Peter could see his toothless grin even in this darkness.

"Steer Nor' West, master. That'll take us up the coast, and if this wind holds we can sail back in the morning. Good night, sah. Good night, masters." The skipper scratched his head as he went below to his quarters. "Jist call if yo want me, masters." With that he disappeared into the darkness of the saloon. The crew, two youngsters in their teens, placed the oil navigation lights in the shrouds and then they disappeared down the forehatch abaft the foremast.

"Lovely night, Brown. What about giving Hawkins the wheel? It's about his turn now." Hank gave Peter a nudge as he went by and strolled for'd. Peter joined the American amidships between the masts where they could whisper safely.

"Nobble the skipper first, Hank, then batten him down in the fore-peak with the others. There's no connection between the fore-peak and the after-quarters, I'm sure. They used to have a bulkhead between the fore-peak and the fish hold, and I shouldn't think things have changed."

"Okay, Skipper, Bill and I'll fix it. This is more up my street!"

They wandered quietly back to the poop and there they explained things to Bill. They could hear snores coming already from the old man below, and then Hank slipped quietly down into the darkness. There was a grunt, a muffled protestation, and then two figures emerged from the hatchway, the skipper's eyeballs rolling in terror in the darkness. It was over in two minutes, the crew battened securely below in the fore-peak.

The youths were still befuddled when they dimly heard a voice calling from the hatchway above: "We're borrowing your ship for a little while, Captain," Peter shouted. "We'll look after her, and if you don't cause trouble, you'll be okay. We'll feed you so you needn't worry; you'll come to no harm if you keep quiet."

A moment of silence and then pandemonium broke out below. Shouting, screaming and cursing, it took a few moments for them to realise what was happening. When Bill returned from inspecting the fish hold, Peter lifted the fore-hatch gingerly. The snorers were fathoms deep…

"You're right, sir," Bill reported. "There's a bulkhead between the fore-peak and the hold. The fore-hatch is the only exit."

"Thanks, Bill," said Peter. "Now, get to your stations, me hearties! We'll go about and run for Trinidad."

Peter slipped aft to the wheel, Hank manned the mainsheets and Bill hustled for'd to the headsails.

"Stand by to go about!"

Peter felt a lump in his throat as he shouted the order. Suddenly life was good. A moment later Bill yelled from the fo'c'sle: "Ready for'd, sir!"

Peter nodded at Hank and then gently put the wheel over. *Moonstone* came up into the wind and hovered momentarily like a bird. The headsails flapped and then her bows paid off. Hand over hand, Hank hauled in the mainsheets, the rigging creaked, and then she paid off on the port tack.

"Let draw!"

The order drifted down on the wind and Hank let the sheets run through his hands. Peter watched the mainsail, and when the boom was coming up against the shrouds he nodded at Hank.

"Well!"

They set the mizzen and, when she was running happily, Peter shouted for Bill.

"Come and take her, Bill, but watch how you go. We mustn't gybe this old lady: we might shake the sticks out of her."

Bill grasped the spokes of the wheel firmly in his hands, and then for the first time in days Peter relaxed as he peered over the transom.

The phosphorescence of the wake sparkled astern. The sea gurgled as it slipped past the old hull. Between the trucks the stars curvetted, twinkling in the indigo of the tropical night. The wavelets curled under her counter and she danced as she bowled before the wind. Hope was possible again and their spirits lifted.

"If this wind holds we'll be off Trinidad in time, men," Peter shouted joyfully. "Let's get below and see if there're any charts on board, Hank. Steer south, Bill."

"Steer south, sir. Aye, aye, sir." Bill coaxed her gently round to the new course. By the yellow light which flickered from the binnacle, Peter could see a smile of contentment creasing the weather-beaten face of the seaman. Peter was glad his old comrade-in-arms was in on this.

They found an old paraffin lamp below, and by its light they rummaged amongst the lockers. There were no charts, but Hank produced a well-thumbed school atlas.

"It'll have to do, I suppose," Peter said, and the atlas fell open at the Caribbean. "I reckon we're about here, Hank." Peter marked their estimated position with a pencilled circle. "We'll steer due south and then we can't be far off the Dragon's Mouth. We should make the passage of the straits tomorrow night, even if the wind drops."

"What speed are you allowing, sir?" Hank asked.

"Averaging three knots. If the wind holds and we get there early, we can always stand off for a few hours and jill about the Gulf of Paria. I think we should make a landfall about here." The pencil marked a cross on the shore not far from the Asphalt Lake. "We'll free the crew when we shove off and land in the dory."

"That means we'll be landing on the morning of the rally, doesn't it, Peter? Liberation Day, they call it."

"Yes — if the wind holds. But you never know out here: there can be a flat calm for weeks on end."

"We've *got* to get there on time, sir." Hank's voice broke. "It's our only chance to save the Bishop and to try and put a spoke in the proceedings."

"Yes, there's still hope. After all, we've got the Sacred Belt. The Serpent King will look pretty stupid because their law won't allow human sacrifice without it. Yakov said that they'd be sacrificing the Bishop, but that was before we pinched the Belt."

"Maybe they haven't tumbled to it yet, sir? We locked the casket up again; at least, we snapped shut the lid."

"All I want to do, Hank, is to land in time near the Asphalt Lake," Peter said. "If we don't, U.N.O. may lose out all the way down the line and we shall forfeit our lives. If we can only get there..." Peter groaned in anguish. "Don't you see, Hank, the whole nightmare depends upon the seduction of the minds of the natives. A sharp jolt and they might return to sanity. They might, you know — you saw for yourself they aren't heart and soul for the Commies."

Hank sat down on the settee and looked up at Sinclair. The Englishman seemed oblivious of the impossible odds: they'd been on the run now for days and they were almost exhausted. Yakov would throw in everything to prevent their escape because, while they remained alive, his whole intelligence network was in jeopardy.

"You know, sir, we're up against it in a big way. Yakov is out to get us. He doesn't like us."

For a moment Peter was angry.

"To blazes with Yakov, Hank! The double-crossing traitor! To think that *Tom Hillyard* fooled us all, especially me, the way he did! We've got to let Bermuda know. We've got to find a way..." Then Peter cooled down. "Sorry, Hank. It's my pride, I suppose. One doesn't like being taken for a ride."

"That's okay, sir," Hank replied softly. "It's Yakov and His Boys versus the Three Musketeers. I wonder how long it'll be before he picks up the trail?"

Peter was dousing the light and then he turned towards the hatchway.

"It depends whether those three policemen rumbled you in St. Georges. If they did, we can expect to be intercepted during the night."

Hank had risen from the settee and was following his Captain up the ladder.

"By what, sir? Aircraft?"

They had reached the deck and the breeze ruffled their hair. It was a dark night and visibility was about three miles.

"I'll take her now, Bill," Peter ordered. "Douse the side lights. Keep a sharp lookout for destroyers. There's one consolation though, Hank," Peter said, as he turned towards the tall figure in the darkness. "This old girl is made of wood and they say that radar isn't nearly so effective on a sailing craft."

"Hope you're right, sir," Hank replied as he moved for'd. "I'll keep watch in the eyes of the ship."

CHAPTER 14

Evening Twilight

The three men shivered in the early dawn. Already *Moonstone* was vanishing from sight as she slid out to sea, her mainsheets belayed while she sailed herself until the native crew had freed itself from the fore-peak. In a few moments she would be lost to sight, and old Johnny would be setting a homeward course for Grenada…

Bill was wringing out the bottoms of his trouser legs. He'd just sunk the dory in the shallows.

"Well, I didn't think we'd make it," Peter whispered. "We're in luck, boys: the destroyers must have searched the wrong area."

"*Moonstone* will take a day or two to reach St. Georges, sir," Hank replied. "I'm glad we had something to eat before landing. I'm hungry."

"We're on time, anyway, sir," Bill said, as he rubbed his hands. "Let's get going, sir. We ain't got much time by all accounts and I want a bit of 'one-one-two'." He flexed his fists and danced on the balls of his feet in the darkness. "We've done all the taking so far. Now for some giving." He grinned, and the ex-Med Fleet champion suddenly let fly with a straight left, followed by a right hook.

"I've still got my shooting-iron anyway," Hank laughed. "I removed it from the guard when I borrowed his uniform."

"That's the only weapon we have between us, so look after it," Peter said, as he started walking up the beach. "We'll strike inland until we meet a road and then we can join up with the locals. They are bound to be up early here. It's devilish hot by midday in Trinidad."

And so by dawn the three men were striding down one of the byroads leading to the Asphalt Lake. It was not difficult to find the way because all roads were signposted, 'To the Rally', and after four hours walking they knew they were near. They had passed only two people, labourers on their way to work at the refinery. A public holiday had been proclaimed, they had said. But they were maintenance men; they had to go to work as usual...

The sun was halfway to its zenith when Peter first saw the lake. They were now on the main road but few people were about yet. They passed a transport park where dozens of vehicles stood idle, trucks that normally worked the day-long, carrying the pitch down to the tankers.

"It's very different from what I remember of my Snotty days," Peter remarked. "The whole business wasn't nearly so organised then. Look at these new roads — they've certainly poured some money in here."

"And taken it out, I guess. It's an American company, don't forget, you guys." Hank was able to laugh at himself. "When are we going to lie up, Pete? My flat feet have had enough."

They were on the edge of the pitch lake and already they could feel the heat reflecting from its surface. Peter walked gingerly on to the asphalt and it was soft underfoot.

They gazed down the length of the lake and at the far end, about a quarter of a mile away, they saw a wooden erection. Bunting was hanging motionless from the scaffolding and it was obvious that this was probably the centre of the day's coming festivities. From the notices along the route, it appeared that the rally was billed to start at seven-thirty in the evening. It would be too hot during the day.

"Come on! Let's get down to the other end and we can lie up on the shore, by those trees opposite the scaffolding," Peter said.

A quarter of an hour later they flopped down in the shade of the few surviving palms. A belt of scrub ran round this end of the lake, and from here they could see without being too conspicuous.

"Food, you guys. Food. I'm off to get some." Hank disappeared towards the row of shacks that ran along the skyline.

"For God's sake, be careful, Hank," Peter called after him. "Don't get caught up in anything now."

Peter and Bill took off their foul shirts and lay resting in the shade of the scrub, each occupied with his own thoughts. Here they were. They'd arrived on time for the rally, but for the life of them they couldn't see what good they could do. How hopeless it all seemed! Three men against thousands, perhaps. Anyway, if the Bishop *was* alive, he'd be brought here for the sacrifice. That stage in the middle was obviously designed for this business. A stake at one end of the platform, a row of petrol drums at the other... Peter shuddered.

"Snap out of it, you guys! Food ... and liquor!" Hank's rumbustiousness jarred. Couldn't the American see the hopelessness of this appalling nightmare? A mob of howling natives would be shrieking for the wretched Bishop's blood soon, and here was Hank, revelling in—

"A bottle of rum, Pete; you have the first swig. Drink to the downfall of our enemies!"

The cork popped, and there Hank stood, rum bottle in hand.

"Look, sir. There's something happening over there. A truck's just drawn up," Bill said quietly.

Hank flopped to the ground and the three men watched the arrival of two jeeps. There was a banging of doors, and a group of Europeans, dressed in khaki uniform, tumbled from the trucks. *Probably police*, Peter thought. A few moments later, shouting and cursing, half a dozen men appeared behind the platform. They were dressed in the khaki shorts and shirts of the local militia and they wore red armbands on their sleeves. A heavily built man seemed to be in charge and he was remonstrating with the others, his raucous voice drifting towards them in the stillness. It was then that Peter saw the broken man in their midst…

Half-dragging and half-carrying the limp figure that slumped in their arms, the brute of an officer kicked continuously at the unconscious man whom they were trying to heave up the steps of the platform. "Get up," the officer was shouting. "We haven't got all day. Come on, get up!" The boot jabbed viciously at the prisoner's stomach.

Peter felt Bill going rigid beside him. He laid a restraining hand upon the seaman's shoulder. "Wait for it," Peter whispered. "Let's see what they do next."

"It's the Bishop, Pete! My God, it's the Bishop!" Hank muttered.

"He's just about out," Peter whispered. "He's got guts!"

The police tied their captive to the stake and then they heard the officer clumping down the steps. "We'll be back before the party starts, MacGrigor. About six-thirty, I should think. So long!" the officer called up to the platform. Then he strode off the lake, taking two of his policemen with him, but leaving three guards behind.

"The jerks!" Hank whispered. "They're adding insult to injury by giving white guards to the black bishop."

"All part of the Communist hate-technique," Peter muttered. "But what are the others up to?"

The three guards were inspecting their prisoner. They adjusted his bonds and then clambered down the steps to the shade beneath the platform. They unslung their packs and settled down to eat.

Peter leaned towards Hank.

"This is our opportunity, Hank. We'll join them for lunch. Lucky you brought the rum: it'll make our job easier." Peter got up and strolled out into the blazing sun. He slouched on to the hot asphalt, his hands thrust deep into his pockets. He wrinkled his eyes as he peered at the guards, and then he whistled towards his two friends in the scrub.

He jerked his head and shouted so that the policemen could hear: "Come on, boys, looks like some fun! Let's eat here!" He shuffled across the yielding surface of the pitch-lake. The tall American, still in the clothes of an officer in the Security Force and wearing a red armband round his right shirt-sleeve, burst from the shade of the trees. He was clutching a rum bottle by its neck and under his other arm a bundle of food was cradled: bread, cheese, a cluster of limes and bananas in a paper bag.

"Hi! Wait for us, Pete! Is that the Black Bishop they've got there?" Loud-mouthed, the tall officer swaggered arrogantly on to the lake. He stood blinking in the sunlight, then marched after the dissolute planter who was swaying towards the wooden platform. Halfway across, the tall officer waited for his other friend to appear. The undergrowth parted, but the latecomer seemed in no hurry. The officer waited impatiently.

"This way, Bill. They've got the man we've been looking for, I reckon," he shouted irritably. It was unbearably hot here — he could feel the heat bouncing off the asphalt underfoot.

The guards were looking suspiciously at the intruders. These three watchdogs had been looking forward to their afternoon's siesta. "What do you want?" the eldest of the three asked Peter. "The show doesn't start till seven-thirty this evening. Clear off."

Peter stopped. He swayed where he stood, his feet astride, eyeing the prisoner on the platform with amusement.

"We want to see the fun, officer, so we got here early. Can we share our food with you? We've got time to kill, and my friend, the officer here," said Peter, jerking his head towards Hank, "he's got a bottle of rum. Won't you have a drink with us?"

The two guards nudged their senior and a smirk spread across the man's dirty, unshaven face.

"Well, that's different…" He moved towards the back of the platform. "Come and join us. We could do with a snort. We've been guarding the old fool for over a week now," he replied as he nodded towards the man at the stake.

"Captain Jefferson and my partner, Mr. Hawkins," Peter introduced. Hank strode up and nearly wrung the senior guard's hand off. "Good to see you," he roared. "We've come a long way for this, bud." He proffered the bottle. "Here, take a nip." Hank flung himself down in the shade under the platform. He relaxed and began to unravel the bundle of food. "Help yourselves, boys. It's too hot for me."

The bottle of rum was soon half empty, and when the luncheon party was at its height Peter noticed the eldest guard nodding. The heat was stifling and Peter was beginning to feel drowsy himself. He winked at Hank, then spoke to the guard: "Before our siesta, my friend, let me see the Bishop. I shan't get such a good chance later on."

A gust of laughter greeted the sally. "We better see that he's not dead with heat exhaustion — it'd be a pity not to have him conscious for the rally, wouldn't it?" Peter watched the implication sink into the befuddled mind. The guard struggled to his feet and lurched into the sunlight. He blinked for a moment in the glare, then stumbled up the wooden steps to the platform, Peter close on his heels.

At the far end of the stage the slumped body of the Bishop hung by its bonds to a vertical pole. Peter watched the guard approach the pathetic figure to peer at the lolling face. The brute yanked the head upwards by its hair, and for the first time Peter saw the Bishop's face. The eyes were closed and puffy, the cheeks bruised, but in spite of this there was grandeur in the massive head, though slumped in semi-consciousness.

The guard let go the hair and the head fell forwards. He threw a fold of the dirty purple cassock over the Bishop's head to protect him in some measure from the sun. Peter strode forward angrily.

"Don't overdo it, man!" he shouted, and he spat derisively. "The man's all right." He snatched the protective covering from the Bishop's head. "Don't mollycoddle the swine. He needs only a bucket of water."

The guard turned towards the planter in surprise. This fellow certainly hated the representative of Christendom, but for all that, he, the custodian, was responsible for the Bishop's safety after all. Then the guard saw the tall man coming towards him.

"Is the fool all right?" the officer asked anxiously.

The guard was relieved to have found an ally.

"Your planter friend seems to think he's all right, but I'm responsible for the prisoner, you know," the man said, now on his dignity. "I daren't let the swine die of sunstroke."

"Let the wretch be, for Pete's sake," Peter exclaimed angrily, and he turned towards the steps. "He's done enough harm, hasn't he?" He walked sulkily away. "Come on, let's get back to the shade." He clambered down the steps. He heard the guard protesting and Hank reassuring the fellow. "My friend's nuts, you know. Let's get below."

In the shade beneath the platform, Peter found Bill sitting on his haunches, and struggling into the shirt of one of the guards whom he had trussed up. Peter winked and they both moved behind the steps. They saw the last guard's feet shuffling down the steps, and as he reached the bottom plank, Peter jumped. He shoved his knee into the man's back, and clapped his hand tight over the mouth. There was a momentary struggle and then the guard lay quiet. His eyes rolled in terror and he grunted as the gag was shoved into his mouth.

"Keep quiet and you'll be all right," Peter hissed. "One squeak from any of you and you're dead ducks. Understand?"

There was a further grunt and they rolled him alongside the other snoring men. "Stay there and get your head down," Bill advised. They stripped the three guards and were soon dressed in their sweat-drenched uniforms. A sodden shirt covered the Sacred Belt which was leaving a pool of moisture around Peter's waist.

"Ugh!" Hank complained. "I don't fancy this."

"Don't be so fussy, Hank," Peter jibed. "You look more the part in this lot, you big galoot!" They laughed at the extraordinary turn of events. "Not a bad fit, sir," Bill exclaimed. "No worse than their owners, anyway."

It was now three-thirty, and the heat was almost unbearable in this airless pocket under the platform.

"Bill," Peter commanded, "hide these three guards behind those empty crates, then peg down the wire netting and hessian running round the platform. We'll have to take a chance on their being discovered. It's my bet that once the show starts, no one will want to look under the stage — there'll be too much petrol about."

"Right, sir. I'll persuade them to keep quiet," he grinned. "I'm not too keen on traitors myself."

"We'll go up top, Hank. Let's see what can be done for the Bishop."

The heat on the platform hit them like a sledgehammer. They could see the waves shimmering across the asphalt, and for a moment Peter's head swam when he reached the top step.

"Quick, sir!" Hank exclaimed behind him. "The first of the crowd's beginning to arrive." He pointed to the far end of the lake where the road ended. A bus had halted there, and a string of gay colours was pouring from it.

Peter had reached the slumped body at the stake. He tore at the bonds.

"Quick, Hank! We've got about ten minutes. Get some water from that drum below. Hurry!"

Hank dashed below and Peter tore the last bight from the prisoner's wrists. If only they'd had longer, they might have been able to get him away! But it was impossible now; they'd have to stick it out on the platform. At least they were with the Bishop.

Supporting the prelate with one hand, Peter loosened the leather belt which held the man's stained cassock together. He heard the clanking of a bucket, and while Peter supported the unconscious man, Hank slopped the tepid water over the man's face and forehead. After several minutes there was still no response.

"For God's sake, hurry up and come round!" Peter swore in desperation. "We've so little time."

The Bishop was a huge man, and Peter was finding his inert weight difficult to support. While Hank was frantically trickling water with a tin lid between the cracked lips, Peter could hear the distant shouts and banter of the approaching firstcomers. The three allies were beaten now. It had been a near thing, but they had lost…

"He's coming round, sir!"

Peter had not noticed the faint quivering of the eyelids. But suddenly his nostrils twitched spasmodically, the lids opened and fluttered, the yellowy-brown whites of his eyes gleamed in their sockets. Then Peter felt the body stiffen as it tried instinctively to take its weight squarely on its feet. Peter gently propped the Bishop against the post, still supporting him with one hand. The cleric stumbled momentarily, stretched and then stood fully upright. He was a gigantic man, an imposing figure of natural dignity: he stood a foot higher than Hank and his enormous chest was like a barrel. The head jerked suddenly as he passed a ham of a hand across his sweating forehead. He looked about him but he was bewildered for a moment. Then he saw his two erstwhile jailers and suddenly his eyes flickered: his enemies were still torturing him, but he gazed upon his tormentors with compassion.

"Leave me alone!" The long arms swept the two guards away. "What do you want now? You know I have nothing to say."

Hank explained rapidly. Peter unclipped the heavy belt from his own waist. It would be safer under the Bishop's cassock, and in a moment he had transferred it beneath the heavy folds of the purple vestment.

The Bishop understood at last, and his hands patted the encumbrance snapped around his waist. "It only just meets," he chuckled in a deep voice. "I've seen the thing, but I never knew I'd be wearing it for my own funeral pyre!" The great brown eyes were twinkling in the manner his flock had once known. "But what now, my friends? If I'm not mistaken, we're a little late. Don't I hear the first of my people, come to see their father-in-God join his Maker?" The Bishop had thrown back his head in an unconscious gesture of defiance. Peter saw the lips moving and overheard the whisper: "God have mercy."

Peter watched the first group of sightseers. They were threading their way along the edge of the lake and were now three hundred yards away. A bunch of youths had run on ahead and their mockings could be heard plainly now.

"Leave it to us, sir," Peter whispered, as he threaded the bonds round the Bishop's hands. "I'm tying you loosely to the stake again, but when the time comes you can slip free. Be ready, sir, ready to do as I say. Now pretend to be unconscious. We shan't leave you." With a few flips of the cord, Peter had bound the huge body to the stake again. "Anything may happen and we'll have to take any chance offered to us. Watch for it, sir, for God's sake."

His head slumped once more to the broad chest and Peter saw the bonds come taut as they took the weight again. The face of the Bishop creased into a smile.

"God will provide, my friends. Even if you have failed, it won't have been in vain."

Hank slipped down the steps to check the rope that ran between the posts driven into the asphalt. This cordon was ten yards from the platform and was supposed to hold back the crowd. Hank drew his baton as the first group of hooligans walked towards him.

"Keep back. No one allowed inside the barrier. The show doesn't start till seven-thirty," Hank shouted.

The youths moved forward in silence. They were in an ugly mood and obviously had been drinking. One of them, a gangling youth in khaki shorts and red shirt, was not going to be put off. He swaggered up to the barrier and leant on the rope, his face within a yard of Hank's.

"It's *our* Freedom Day, not yours, white trash! We've come to see the traitor. Who's going to stop us?"

Hank's baton flashed in the sun. The youth's hands shot upwards; he grunted and slumped to the ground.

"I am."

There was no doubting Hank's determination. The youths scuttled away and gathered themselves together out of harm's way, preparing to rush Hank. Peter strode to the edge of the platform, legs astride, hands on hips.

"Take your friend with you, boys!" he yelled. "Reinforcements are arriving at any minute, so don't annoy the police. Go and wait in the shade. Clear off until the proper time."

For a moment it was touch and go. If Hank drew his pistol now, that would finish their chances. The youths whispered together. Then two of them rushed forward and quickly dragged their moaning chum after them. Peter and Hank were relieved to see them slink off to the shade at the edge of the lake. Bill stepped up behind Peter and they both saw Hank grinning up at them.

"Keep your shooting-iron until the last resort, Hank."

"Right, Pete. But mebbe it'll be a bit tricky holding back this mob until seven-thirty."

The heat was less oppressive now. The early birds, once they had seen there was to be no nonsense with the three guards, soon settled down on their haunches behind the cordon. The women arrived first, their children pattering after. Soon all was scurry, chatter and laughter ... a dog fight, laughing children playing 'tag', and hiding behind their mothers' skirts. Melons and food appeared and village picnics spread across the asphalt. Hank and Bill had their work cut out holding the crowd back from the rope, but there was no more trouble as the cool of the evening began to soothe the milling humanity.

Peter remained upon the platform... From the corner of his eye he watched the crowd multiplying below him. He watched with amusement as Bill tried to console a distraught mother who had lost her child. She was nursing a baby in her plump arms, whilst the remainder of her brood clung to her skirts, wailing at the top of their little lungs. It was a relief to see Bill holding the prodigal by the hand. All went well from then onwards. After a few ribaldries at the first sight of their Bishop, the newcomers would squat down and concentrate on their food.

Peter was watching like a lynx. He was certain that most of the mocking, particularly from the more responsible elements in the crowd, was more for the benefit of their friends, than any act of hate. He couldn't be sure, but surely there were some who looked and felt ashamed.

They had loved their prelate, he was certain. The Bishop had been renowned in the Antilles for his lovable personality and homely touch; he had spared no pains to alleviate their miserable poverty.

It was simpler to hate, but it was with shame that they did so when they saw their beloved Bishop hanging unconscious from that stake. Peter could hear the professional agitators mingling with the crowd and it made his blood boil to listen to the lies spouting from their lips. The Serpent King and the fetish of the Sacred Belt were stronger bonds at the moment. He shuddered when he heard a man howling for blood.

He looked at his watch — seven-twenty. Time had dragged unbearably. The shadows were beginning to lengthen across the edge of the lake when Bill unobtrusively visited the trussed-up guards beneath the platform. But their bonds and gags were secure, and they were fast asleep; unless some idiot went poking about down underneath the stage, there was no danger from them.

Peter felt trapped by circumstances. They could not escape with the Bishop now, and all they could do was to seize any opportunity that came their way. The agony of waiting was making them fidgety … if only the climax would come, they could face up to it. He felt numbed at the prospect of imminent death; it was strange how resigned he felt.

CHAPTER 15

Light of Day

Peter jumped at the roar of the motorcycles. Then he heard the trucks and cars grinding to a standstill along the road at the head of the lake. *The first of the escort*, he thought, and his heart sank as he beckoned Hank and Bill to rejoin him on the platform. They had been dreading this moment for hours and now time had run out.

Peter slowly moved towards the figure at the stake. He toyed with the bonds while he waited for the crowd to be distracted by the entrance of its King. Hank was standing by him now and Peter muttered for a knife. He felt the steel sliding into his hand, and when he heard the crowd groping to its feet, he whispered to the Bishop:

"The Serpent King's arriving, sir. Take the weight yourself and lean against the post. I'm cutting the knot now. Don't move away from the post or the rope will fall off. God bless you, sir."

Hank and Bill were standing close to the victim, shielding him from the crowd who were straining to glimpse the arrival of their King. With a swift movement, the blue steel flashed and the rope was severed at the vital knot. One heave of the broad shoulders and the Bishop could burst free.

"You're clear now, sir," Peter whispered. "But don't move yet. We'll not leave you." Peter was choking with emotion. The man's head remained slumped on his chest, but Peter heard him grunt an acknowledgement. The vast frame slowly spread its shoulders and leant firmly against the post as the Bishop took his weight squarely upon his feet.

"I'm going to douse you with water when the King mounts the platform," Peter warned in a whisper, "but try not to move, sir."

Bill had moved unnoticed towards the petrol drums at the other end of the stage. Hank faced the top of the steps. Peter heard the sound of marching men approaching from behind and he turned round slowly.

A hundred yards away two platoons of Militia were swinging towards the platform. He identified the same officer who had delivered the Bishop here earlier in the day, and Peter's heart sank. If they were to be recognised as impostors now, that would be '*finis*' ... they'd be torn limb from limb, publicly lynched by the mob now milling below them in its thousands. He kept a sharp eye on the officer who was disposing his men around the roped-off area encircling the platform. The militia captain had his work cut out because the crowd was now in jocular mood, bustling to get a better view near the front. Peter moved nearer Hank:

"Hank — if that swine starts coming up here, you've got to stop him at the bottom of the steps. Take him underneath and fix him. It's our only chance or he'll recognise us. Here's the knife." He slipped the steel back into Hank's outstretched fingers. Hank grunted. He descended the steps and disappeared.

Bill was strolling up and down the platform when Peter first felt the gaze of the platoon officer. He turned slowly and found the man watching him intently. Peter came smartly to attention and saluted.

For a moment the man seemed satisfied. But as Peter averted his head again, he caught sight of the fellow forcing his way through the crowd in his haste to reach the stairway at the back of the platform. Peter felt the skin prickling at the back of his neck. If Hank bungled it... Peter walked to the back of the platform and turned his back on the crowd. The officer could not see him here.

Suddenly there was a shout near the palm trees. Someone had seen the first of the royal cars arriving, and the welcome was taken up by thousands of expectant throats. The roar was spine-chilling and lasted for a full three minutes as the resplendent cortège was identified. In the clamour, Peter heard a muffled shot from below the platform and he gasped. He turned towards the stairway. The top of a uniformed cap was slowly ascending. Peter retreated towards the Bishop, poised upon the balls of his feet and ready to spring. Slowly the head appeared ... and then Hank was staring at him, calm and serious.

Peter felt his heart thumping below his shirt and his hands were trembling. Hank walked to the other end of the platform, turned, and then came slowly up to Peter.

"I killed him."

Peter nodded. They were safe for a few moments longer, for now a bevy of police was clearing a path towards the stage. He could hear the whine of American-type sirens and the crowd howled with delight. There was a sudden rush towards the front of the rope and he saw the guards linking arms to prevent the cordon from giving way.

"Here they come, Peter. This is it," Hank said, loosening the gun in its holster.

Peter turned towards the entrance. Walking majestically between two rows of militia, a huge man was striding. He towered above his entourage and Peter recognised him as the same fanatical figure he'd seen haranguing the crowds in St.

Lucia. But now he was more resplendently attired: wearing a cloak of gold and crimson brocade, gleaming gold encircled his head; he held a long sceptre, and this he raised in stately acknowledgement of the crowd's acclamations. Following close behind came four retainers, each with a corner of the heavy casket of the Sacred Belt resting on his shoulder. This party was surrounded by a close circle of troops, but Peter gasped when he recognised the leader of the next squad.

"Yakov's here, Hank. Tell Bill to turn the other way." He turned quickly himself, his back towards the advancing cortège. Hank moved close to Bill, then all three were facing the crowd. Even above the hilarious uproar Peter could feel his heart pounding. Should Yakov join the royal party on the platform, they were sunk…

A military band had added its quota now and the cacophony became tumultuous. The thumping drums and shrill bugles burst through the martial music. Then Peter felt the Serpent King mounting the stairway behind him and the stage rocked with the extra weight of milling bodies. The King had arrived and he stood in the centre of the platform, glorying in this moment. Peter bowed low from the waist, keeping his face averted.

From the corner of his eye, Peter watched the great man, and then he saw the casket being placed on a wooden plinth that had been carried up. The casket was to the left of centre, the hasp facing the crowd so that all could see when it was opened. The privileged escort who carried the casket stood back. Peter could hear no others mounting the stairway. The stage was set for the King.

Peter slowly turned round and then, to his immense relief, he saw the Communist hierarchy being shepherded along the lake to the other side of the platform. He couldn't see Yakov for the overhang of the staging, but Bill would have to move quickly if he wasn't to be recognised. Mercifully he saw Bill slipping down the back of the stage, and then all the three friends were together, within a yard of the prisoner at the stake.

The crowd hushed as the King advanced to the front of the platform while the four retainers hustled three swan-necked microphones in front of him. The King lifted his arms and the folds of the gorgeous robe rustled in the silence.

The Serpent King began quietly, as he had done in Castries. In a gesture of submissive obedience, the crowd fell to its knees and Peter heard the rustle of the movement far into the darkness. Twilight was over now and silvery green streaks were threading across the western sky.

"Light your torches, brothers."

The silky bass voice issued its first command, and then pinpoints of light started flickering like glow-worms at Peter's feet. The torches on the platform were lit by the casket guards, and suddenly Peter could see no longer the sea of faces in front of them. He found himself being bewitched by the hysteria of the night and he had to shake his head quickly. He saw Hank finger his pistol in its holster beneath the shirt, and he watched Bill moving to the other side of the stake. Peter stood sentinel immediately behind the Bishop.

"Rouse the traitor!"

The command boomed out clearly over the loudspeakers. A roar of delight sprang from thousands of throats as the King pointed dramatically towards the slumped body at the stake. Peter stepped forward. He picked up the bucket and splashed the contents full in the face of the Bishop.

The enormous head shook for a second, then came slowly erect. He gazed in compassion towards the populace beneath him. He was blinded, but in the flickering light Peter could see that he was fully awake. Peter retreated behind the stake, and as he did so, he whispered in the Bishop's ear: "Stand by, sir. We'll make a break for it if we have to."

His head nodded once, and then turned towards his tormentor. He remained silent as the King pointed accusingly towards him.

"Here, O brothers, is your sacrifice for tonight; the night you have all been living for; this night that heralds your Day of Freedom. Tomorrow we take over the whole island, the whole Federation. This is your night of Freedom, my brothers." Now the King's voice had risen as he turned again to his audience.

Slowly the King whipped up the crowd to a frenzy, a note of shrill hysteria creeping into his voice. He was playing with them now, a smile hovering at the corners of his lips. He reminded them of their past, of the indignities they had suffered for centuries, of their new masters who were here to help them throw off the yoke that had burdened them so long.

Peter heard the voice growing shriller, more primeval, until his ears sang with the nightmare quality of this hypnotic spellbinder. He watched the crowd stamping its feet below him and heard the howls of eagerness as the time for sacrifice drew nearer.

Peter shook himself again as he felt a lump rising in his throat. Did the King realise the casket was full of sand? Was he going to kill the prisoner without going through the ceremonial of offering the Sacred Belt? Surely he would not dare ignore the custom of centuries: the Belt had to be presented before human sacrifice was carried out. He began to feel uneasy.

He jumped back when a lighted brand landed suddenly on the platform. Some enthusiast had hurled it on to the stage, and then Hank stamped on the torch. It went out, and the smoke from it smouldered at their feet, choking them. Hank kicked it gently towards the King.

"The Sacred Belt! The Belt! Show us the Sacred Belt!"

Now the clamour was taken up by the mob and Peter shuddered. His spine tingled as he recognised murder in the air. He laid his hand on the Bishop's shoulder.

For a second, the King looked towards his victim. The Bishop was staring him straight in the eye, but the King could not meet the good man's gaze. *The Christians in the Roman arena must have faced death like this*, Peter thought to himself, and suddenly he was afraid no longer. If the Bishop were to die, they'd perish with him… He felt strangely at peace.

"Put on the Belt. Wear the Sacred Belt, O King!"

The clamour was more consistent now, demanding, compelling. Perhaps the King had overreached himself and the crowd was master now?

The King raised his arms. There was a sudden lull and he pointed towards the casket on his left.

"Open it!" he commanded, and his voice boomed round the arena.

The four guards leapt forwards. Three held the box while the fourth moved to the front. He turned his back on the crowd and Peter saw him banging the front of the box with his fist. Peter held his breath … then the hasp sprang open. The man jumped clear and, as he moved to the rear, his companions lifted the lid…

The silence seemed eternal. The guards lifted the casket. As was the custom, they lifted it forwards for the crowd to gaze on the glittering fetish. It was death for anyone to view it at any moment other than at a sacrificial ceremony, and now all eyes were watching the casket as it tilted forwards. Peter heard the intake of breath from those on the platform and he looked at the dancing sea of faces gazing upwards… He turned towards the casket himself and held his breath as he watched.

"Stand by, Hank — Bill…"

A trickle of shining sand ran slowly from the sloping casket; it was a few moments before the guards realised what was happening: the casket high above their heads and the sand cascading from it. Not until the trickle had increased to an avalanche did they lower the box. The crowd had seen it happen before their eyes.

In the ominous silence, the Serpent King leapt towards the casket. He buried his hand in the pyramid of sand at his feet and scooped up a handful. He spread his fingers and, fascinated, he watched it trickle through.

The tension was electric. Peter felt his heart thumping against his ribs as he looked at the King. The first murmurings of dissatisfaction and unbelief were rumbling through the mob. Their King had tricked them. Something was amiss: he'd lost the Sacred Belt and now there could be no sacrifice. The shouting and the clamour grew and Peter saw the guards fighting in the torchlight to hold back the front row of onlookers. But the flood from behind was becoming overwhelming…

The Serpent King spun round to face the Bishop. In the sudden hush, the crowd watched the two antagonists. The King in the centre of the platform, frozen for a moment in time, his mouth open, his hand outstretched accusingly; the Bishop gazing calmly at him, his head defiant, his eyes unyielding.

Suddenly the tableau shattered. The massive bulk of the Bishop, robed in purple splendour, seemed to burst its bonds. They saw him stretch his chest, spread his arms, and then the ropes fell miraculously to the planking. The mob gasped, and a woman's shriek pierced the stillness. He heard the crowd shuffling backwards, like the whisper of poplar leaves on a summer's evening.

They saw the Serpent King retreat, his eyes glinting wickedly. They watched the Bishop, the man they had once loved so well, the man who had confirmed them and their children, advance upon the King who had tricked them. The Bishop's eyes were blazing as he stepped towards the microphones, thrusting the King aside. His head lifted in all its grandeur and there he stood, his left arm by his side, his right hand raised in blessing. In the hush, Peter heard the faint sobbing of women and then a man began to shout at the back of the crowd.

The Bishop moved his right hand and for a second fumbled beneath his cassock. There was a flash and there in front of him hung the Sacred Belt, glinting in the torchlight. All eyes stared at it and men gasped as they saw the deep glow of rubies.

The rich voice summoned the multitude and, as they watched, some sank to their knees. The Belt flashed again and they saw their Bishop raise it with his right hand. He flicked the Belt then, as a man kills a snake by snapping its back. The jewels and the gold glinted and then something fell to the platform. There remained only half the Belt in his hand. He flung this to the ground with the piece that lay at the Serpent King's feet.

"See the power of God, my children!"

A sigh rustled through the crowd. Now the men were sinking to their knees as they watched the guards cringing against the rear of the platform. They saw the Serpent King snatch up the brand that had lain at his feet. He peered quickly towards the torches at the back of the platform and his intention was clear: he would plunge the brand into the petrol drum which stood at the left-hand edge of the stage, ignite it from the torches flickering at the back of the stage, then set the Bishop afire. Like lightning, with a scythe-like sweep before Hank could pounce, he'd snatched the brand from the planks. Then he plunged it into the petrol drum.

No one realised what happened next, events moved so rapidly: there was a flash, an explosion and a sheet of flame. Then they saw the figure of the Serpent King, ablaze, on fire from head to foot, himself a living torch. For a split second he stood motionless, rooted to the spot by shock; he gazed down in disbelief at his flaming hands; then he rushed to the back of the platform, a brand of streaming fire. He leaped into the darkness, a shrieking, horrified man, to crash to the ground below. His guards jumped after him, and Peter heard them rolling him over in the dirt, smothering the flames. The cries stopped, and in the shocked silence all that could be heard was the low moaning of a reprieved man.

When the Bishop first started speaking through the microphones, he had for his background accompaniment the subsiding moans of his adversary, an adversary who represented all that was hateful in a modern dictatorship.

Men, women and children gazed upon their beloved Bishop. They had loved him before, but never had they worshipped him like this. He truly reflected the glory of God, his deep voice ringing out clearly and proudly through the silent, receptive humanity. He reminded them of their faith, of the years they had shared together. He recalled the difficult times and how they had endured them together. Men were kneeling around the perimeter of the stage and Peter saw that they were weeping silently. The Bishop gently called them to prayer and Peter watched as Hank and Bill fell to their knees on the rostrum. Peter dropped to the rough planking and then he heard the Absolution being pronounced in the deep, sonorous tones of the man of God. The Bishop stood back from the microphones. He subsided to his knees and bowed his head.

Peter watched the women in the front of the crowd. They were groping for their children and their menfolk, and he saw them smiling into each other's eyes while the tears streamed down their faces. It had been a long time since first they had strayed, but now they had found their shepherd to guide them home. It had been a long, long journey which had so nearly ended in disaster…

Then in the far distance Peter heard a deep bass voice. The clear notes resonated in ringing tones in the night, and Peter found his soul leaping in exultation as he listened to the words that came streaming forth, words that had been sung in village, town and harbour for so many years

"… marching as to war,
With the Cross of Jesus…"

And then the refrain was taken up by the crowd in the distance, until the singing finally reached the ranks below the platform. Peter saw the shining faces looking upwards and then the crowd surged towards its saviour. They swept on to the stage and carried him off in their strong hands. They took him away and put him down gently by the edge of the platform. Slowly, silently, they ushered him to the head of the motley procession, the torches lighting the way before him. As he started walking, the round face was peering up at his rescuers on the platform. He moved slowly past the three friends, his right hand held aloft in benison. They could see his lips moving, his face glistening from the tears that streamed unchecked down his cheeks. They heard the crashing and the thumping of the Christian marching song and then imperceptibly the lake slowly emptied of humanity. The Secret

Police had long since fled, the militia had been withdrawn, the nightmare suddenly over. The West Indians had returned once more to the faith of their fathers and sanity ruled once more in their hearts.

The torches were still spluttering in their holders at the rear of the platform when Peter turned to his two friends. It was only then that Peter realised that both Hank and Bill too were still on their knees.

The faint notes of 'Onward, Christian Soldiers' were dying away to the southward now. The fading hues of another tropical sunset were fast disappearing. The palms rustled their leaves at the edge of the lake. Peter rose to his feet and went towards his two comrades. They put their arms round each other's shoulders and slowly descended the wooden stairway.

EPILOGUE

An unobtrusive announcement appeared in *The Times* three days later, dated 27th May:

H.M. Nuclear Submarine Rugged *berthed today at Port of Spain, Trinidad. She has been on routine United Nations patrols, and is now paying a courtesy visit to the capital of this island. According to our Special Correspondent, her stay is expected to last somewhat longer than anticipated and local leave has been granted to her ship's company.*

GLOSSARY

A.M.C. — Armed Merchant Cruiser.

ASDIC — The device by which submarines are detected. Submarines are also fitted with this device, when it is used as a hydrophone.

BAG — Slang for prisoner-of-war camp.

BARRACK-STANCHION — A man who manages to secure for himself a permanent appointment in a shore station.

BEARING — The direction of an object.

BLOWERS — Machines which blow out the water in the tanks of a submarine by using low-pressure air.

BOX — The main batteries.

BUNCH OF BANANAS — Slang for aiguillettes.

CORTICENE — A type of heavy linoleum used to cover the steel deck.

CRACK — To open a valve quickly, and to shut it immediately.

D.A. — Direction Angle (torpedo-firing angle).

D.R. — Dead Reckoning.

E-BOAT — The fast enemy motor-torpedo boat.

FIFTH-COLUMNISTS — Traitors working inside one's own society.

FIN — The conning tower of a nuclear submarine.

FREE FLOOD — The open holes in the casing and tanks through which the water enters freely.

FRUIT MACHINE — A metal box into which all relevant attack data is fed, and from which the necessary information is extracted to carry out an attack.

GASH — Garbage.

GRATICULE — The fine centre-line and range calibrations which are marked on the lens of the periscope.

GROUP DOWN — Low speed on the main electric motors, thus using up little electric power.

GROUP UP — High speed on the main electric motors, thus using up the battery power quickly.

GUFF — A squirt of H.P. air.

H.E. — Hydrophone Effect, i.e., propeller noise.

H.E. — High explosive.

HEADS — Lavatory.

HEAT — Slang for a submarine at the receiving end of a severe depth-charge attack.

H.P. — High Pressure.

H.S.D. — Higher Submarine Detector; the rank of a skilled Asdic operator.

LAYER — A difference of temperature gradients in the ocean.

MAIN BALLAST KINGSTON — Water is allowed to enter into the internal tanks amidships through the Kingston valves.

MAIN BALLAST TANKS — The tanks which give the submarine its buoyancy. All are fitted with main vents, numbers 1 and 6 being external, the remainder internal.

MAIN VENTS — The large mushroom valves on the top of the Main Ballast tanks. When the main vents are open water will rush into the tanks; but, if the main vents are shut, the air cannot escape when the Main Ballast tanks are blown, because the 'blow' is at the top of the tank and the free-flood holes at the bottom. Water is therefore forced through the holes in the bottom of the tank, H.P. air taking its place.

OLD MAN — Slang for Captain.

OUTSIDE E.R.A. — The Engine Room Artificer whose duty is at the panel in the Control Room, and who is therefore 'outside' the Engine Room.

PERISHER — Slang for Commanding Officers' Qualifying Course.

PIFFLE-WURFER — A capsule representing a submarine-contact which can be ejected by a submarine to confuse a destroyer's counter-attack.

PING-RUNNING — Acting as a 'clockwork mouse' to provide a target for training destroyers.

PRESSURE HULL — The cigar-shaped hull of a submarine which is tested to the safe diving depth. If any part of this structure is pierced, the submarine is unlikely to survive.

'Q' TANK — The emergency tank for quick diving. When flooded, this extra water makes the submarine ten tons heavier than her normal dived trim. After diving, this extra water is blown out of 'Q' tank by high-pressure air. If this tank is required to be flooded when dived, its vent has merely to be opened to allow the air in the tank to be vented either inboard or outboard, when the sea will rush into 'Q'. In wartime, 'Q' tank is always kept flooded when the submarine is on the surface.

SNOTTY — Midshipman.

STICK — Slang for periscope.

THROWERS — A type of mortar mounted on the quarterdecks of destroyers. When fired they hurl depth charges well clear of each quarter.

U-BOAT — Enemy submarine of any nationality.

UCKERS — The sailor's version of 'Ludo'.

URSULA SUIT — Waterproof overalls in general use, designed by the Commanding Officer of H.M. Submarine *Ursula*.

A NOTE TO THE READER

Dear Reader,

If you have enjoyed the novel enough to leave a review on **Amazon** and **Goodreads**, then we would be truly grateful.

Sapere Books is an exciting new publisher of brilliant fiction and popular history.

To find out more about our latest releases and our monthly bargain books visit our website: **saperebooks.com**

Printed in Great Britain
by Amazon

59378850R00129